'An adventure so thrilling it makes time fly!' BEN MILLER, author of THE BOY WHO MADE THE WORLD DISAPPEAR

'A time-travel mystery that mana masterminds, neurodivergence, racia friendships *and* Samuel Johnson – all narrated in Elle's exuberant and energetic voice. Even better than *The Infinite*! Loved it!' FLEUR HITCHCOCK, author of THE BOY WHO FLEW

'A gripping time-travel story that keeps you guessing' CHRIS BONNELLO, author of UNDERDOGS

'Chock-full of wicked wordplay and time-travelling conundrums, but also a breathlessly paced thriller' STEVE TASANE, author of CHILD I

'*The Time-Thief* pulses to its own thrillingly original beat. An exhilarating, intelligent and twisty time-travelling mystery' SINÉAD O'HART, author of THE EYE OF THE NORTH

'Wonderfully imaginative . . . fun, exciting and tells you something about 1752 you absolutely need to know' LINDA BUCKLEY-ARCHER, author of THE GIDEON TRILOGY

'*The Time-Thief* plays with time the way a watchmaker creates a watch: with ingenuity and invention' GEOFF ALLNUTT, co-author of the AHS Women and Horology Project

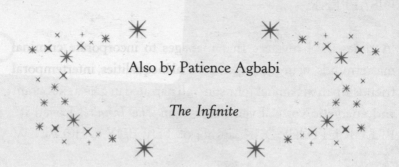

Also by Patience Agbabi

The Infinite

THE TIME-THIEF

PATIENCE AGBABI

CANONGATE

First published in Great Britain in 2021 by Canongate Books Ltd,
14 High Street, Edinburgh EH1 1TE

canongate.co.uk

1

British Library Cataloguing-in-Publication Data
A catalogue record for this book is available on
request from the British Library

ISBN 978 1 78689 990 3

Typeset in Horley Old Style MT by Palimpsest Book Production Ltd,
Falkirk, Stirlingshire

Printed and bound in Great Britain by Clays Ltd, Elcograf S.p.A.

LEXICO'GRAPHER. *n.s.*
[λεξιχὸυ and γφάφω; *lexicographe*, French.]
A writer of dictionaries; a harmless
drudge, that busies himself in tracing
the original, and detailing the signification
of words.

– Dr Johnson

Thirty days hath September,
April, June and November.
All the rest have thirty-one,
Excepting February alone,
Which hath twenty-eight days clear
And twenty-nine in each leap year.

– Anon

To Jeremy, for reminding me that history is not what happened but a *story* of what happened.

Contents

∞ Chapter 01:00 ∞

STOP, THIEF!

It's summer solstice, the longest day, Monday the 21st of June 2021. The sun rose at 4:43 this morning and won't set till 9:21 this evening. Today, I'm going on a school trip to the Museum of the Past, the Present and the Future. I'm so excited that I got up with the sun and couldn't eat any breakfast even though Grandma woke early to cook it.

I place the mozzarella onto the white flatbread, fold it and squeeze it into my white lunchbox. As I close the lid, Grandma stops my hand.

'Elle, this your cheese sandwich not enough. Pack some fruit-o!'

'There's no time to chop the apple, Grandma. We'll be late.'

I look at my best friend, Big Ben, who is sitting at our table. He's just finished eating MY breakfast, fish fished from the pepper soup with fresh boiled yam, and he didn't cough once! He's already had porridge and two slices of toast at home. He doesn't usually collect me from The Mush-Rooms before school

1

but today's a special day and demands the special-day routine. We have to leave at 8:25 exactly. I won an annual poetry competition and I'm going to read my poem at the museum. I'm nervous as well as excited but if we stick to the special-day routine, it will help me stay calm.

Grandma does big-eyes.

'Leapling never late.'

I smile. She has a point. Big Ben and I are both Leaplings with The Gift, which means we were born on the 29th of February and have the ability to leap through time to any year, date or hour we want. Only a tiny percentage of Leaplings have The Gift. Those Leaplings and their families all swear the Oath of Secrecy to protect us from exploitation. If bad Annuals found out about our Gift, they might kidnap us and make us commit crimes that the normal police would never detect. We must be discreet when we leap and reserve our talent for when it's absolutely necessary. Leaping takes it out of you.

Grandma pulls a transparent fruit carton out of the fridge.

'White grapes,' she pretends to read.

I smile at her joke. Grandma can't read but she hopes I'll eat them if it SAYS the grapes are white even though, strictly speaking, they're green. Only Grandma can get away with that. I'm autistic and she knows wordplay's one of my favourite things ever. I mainly eat white food, otherwise I get sensory overload from the sight, smell and taste of it. But over the past few months my sensory issues have been less severe and I've been a bit more confident trying new things, so I think maybe I'll let her pack

2

them today. I nod and she begins washing the grapes under the cold tap.

'My Chronophone says 8:22,' says Big Ben.

He's autistic too and loves to time things. Thank goodness he said that – I almost forgot to pack my own phone. I turn from Grandma to run my hand under the sofa bed where I sleep and there it is, my silver Chronophone. It's just like a mobile phone, but it can send messages across time. Holding it, I remember my leap-birthday celebration at this table last year when Big Ben and I were 3-leap, which is 12, and our friends MC^2 and GMT were 4-leap, 16. That's when MC^2 gave me and Big Ben these special phones. They weren't a birthday present. We helped break up a crime ring working under Le Temps, who took orders from the big bad boss, Millennia. Millennia's old and well-spoken and looks respectable but she's evil incarnate and threatened to DESTROY me. The Chronophones marked our status as Level 1 Infinites.

I LOVE being an Infinite. The Infinites are a youth group who fight crimes on the timeline for a better, greener future. We work for Infinity but no one's ever seen her! Our symbol is the infinity sign: ∞. We each have a code name based on our real name. When you say Elle, it sounds exactly the same as my code name: L. This is all TOP SECRET. Promise you won't tell anyone!

I pack my Chronophone and lunchbox into my rucksack and Big Ben stands up. He's so tall and Grandma's so small, it's like he's twice her size. Grandma hugs me extra tight because she's so proud I won the poetry competition and knows I'm

3

nervous with excitement about reading my poem. She waves at Big Ben. As the two of us walk down the stairs, I hear her voice behind me.

'Be strong and of a good courage,' she says.

∞

It's the first day of Time-Travel Week when we're off school timetable for five days. We won't LITERALLY travel through time every day; sometimes it's workshops where we think outside time and space. Big Ben and I reach school at 8:55 so we're not late but everyone else attending the trip is already outside on the school field.

We're the only two day-pupils; all the other children are boarders. Jake and Maria wave us over. Jake's brown fringe is longer than ever and his freckles stand out more in the summer. Maria's just had her long black hair cropped short so she doesn't have to tie it up when she high jumps. We sit down with them on the grass, which is already dry. It's going to be a very hot day.

I'm in Eighth Year at Intercalary International now. The whole class and three grown-ups are assembled: Mrs C Eckler, Mr C Eckler and Mrs Grayling. Mrs C Eckler, my form tutor, teaches Past, Present and Future (aka PPF) so she arranged the trip and I can tell she's nervous because she keeps twiddling the flower in her pinned-up ginger hair; Mr C Eckler's coming to help out, wearing his sunglasses as usual but at least it's summer; and Mrs Grayling teaches maths, is tall and strong like a javelin thrower

4

and loves the year 1752. She's been there so many times she keeps bumping into different versions of herself. Which must hurt!

As we're a large group and it's sunny and dry, Mrs C Eckler says leaping from the school field is better than leaping from Block T. Block T's the only school building you can leap from and to. The rest of the school is coated with Anti-Leap, a special material used for the prison and other important Leapling buildings to stop people breaking in or breaking out. It can be activated or deactivated like an alarm. Here it's supposed to protect pupils from Leapling intruders at all times. It's also supposed to stop pupils leaping away but I managed to do it last year by mistake!

Mrs C Eckler checks we all have a packed lunch then makes us stand to form a Chrono, a circle for leaping.

'It's summer solstice. We can pretend to be the standing stones of Stonehenge.'

Stonehenge is Mrs C Eckler's favourite place ever. She says it's best at winter solstice when it's dark and cold and quiet. At summer solstice there are too many tourists. I check my watch. It's 9:00. My hair is cornrowed tightly against my head and I'm wearing my long-sleeved white tunic and matching trousers to keep me cool. All eighteen of us hold hands in the Chrono. Big Ben's on my right; Mrs C Eckler's on my left. Big Ben sneezes and I feel sorry for him being outside in the field in the middle of summer. His hayfever gets quite bad but thankfully he's OK when he's running or leaping. Mrs C Eckler makes sure I'm wearing my leap band so I don't get leapsickness. It works like a travel-sickness wristband but looks like a gold bangle.

5

'Close your eyes, everyone,' she says, 'and concentrate on the Museum of the Past, the Present and the Future. Allow us to guide you to the landing spot.'

She means the adults. None of us pupils have been to the museum before. I feel my body go fizzy with energy and squeeze Big Ben's hand tight. He enjoys the excitement of leaping and so do I, but my sensitivities kick in so I always find it challenging. Hopefully the leap band will work this time. At least it's only leaping through space, not through space and time. Mrs C Eckler clears her throat.

'We've arrived. That only took a few seconds. Well done, everyone. You may open your eyes but please remain holding hands.'

I slowly open my eyes and blink. Our circle is surrounded by a much larger circle of stones obviously based on Stonehenge, except these stones look like giant ice cubes. Not the clear ice cubes you'd put in a drink, they're cloudier than that, but not totally white like snow blocks either. They dazzle so brightly, I have to squint to appreciate them. They look like they're melting in the sun but when I touch one, it's totally dry. Then I get it. This is an outdoor sculpture to symbolise global warming.

∞

Our visit will begin in the 1752 Gallery, which is in the basement. The museum arranges everything by floor, so when you enter at ground level it's The Present, which changes annually, then each level you go up, it gets more futuristic. They even have a

Chronophone that an explorer brought back from 2440; it's made of materials no one's invented yet! Big Ben starts to climb the spiral staircase two steps at a time with his long legs because he's excited about the far future artefacts but I pull him back. We have to follow the plan and the tour begins with the past. I look down at page one of the itinerary; I'm on it!

9:15 *The 1752 Gallery Introduction*: Mrs Zhong

9:25 *The Story of an Object*: Anno (Music, Maths and Movement School)

9:30 *1752 Poetry Prize Presentation (2021)*: Elle Ifiè (Intercalary International School)

Big Ben and I jog down the spiral staircase, which is a bit naughty because you're not allowed to run in a museum, but we're athletes so we sometimes forget we're not in training! We slow down before we reach the bottom stair. The 1752 Gallery is circular, its walls lined with objects in glass cases like teapots and snuff boxes and hanging ballads, poems they sang about prisoners to entertain the crowd before they were hung! But the museum assistants don't make us sit in a circle, they make us sit in rows like in school, in case we accidentally hold hands in a Chrono and end up in another time and place! I don't think they trust schoolchildren very much. I'm glad when they leave the room to go back to their offices.

The first session begins. The curator, Mrs Zhong, is small, wearing a black skirt suit and heavy black-rimmed glasses. She looks stern and has a slight accent.

'Welcome to the 1752 Gallery. As you may know, 1752 was a very special leap year. Raise your hands if you know why.'

'The 11-day leap,' says Jake, without putting his hand up.

Mrs Zhong frowns at his disobedience. 'Could anyone tell me the significance of the 11-day leap?'

I know the answer. On Wednesday September the 2nd 1752, EVERYONE in England leapt 11 days into the future! That night, Leaplings and Annuals went to bed and when they woke up, it was Thursday September the 14th! Leaplings didn't hold hands in a Chrono and transport all the Annuals in the middle like luggage. This was a leap by law. The government changed from the Julian to the Gregorian calendar and to make it work, they cut 11 days in time!

But I don't put my hand up to say this out loud because I'm so nervous about doing my reading. If I speak, the words will come out in the wrong order or jammedtogetherinonelongword-likeGerman.

I zone out of the discussion until Mrs Zhong says something about 1752 being the favourite holiday destination for Leaplings with The Gift and notices Big Ben has raised his hand.

'Is that why Mrs Grayling goes there 23 times in 10 years?'

I look at Mrs Grayling. She's gone bright pink but she's smiling, knowing Big Ben didn't mean to be unkind. Everyone knows she's been to 1752 a lot but Big Ben's the only one who's kept tabs whenever she's spoken about it. He must be feeling relaxed to ask a question in a place he's never visited before. Mrs C Eckler twiddles her hair flower.

'Perhaps, Mrs Grayling, you could tell the children about the Carnival of the Calendar.'

Mrs Grayling is a paler shade of pink now. 'Very well, since my secret's out. I visit 1752 to attend an event on the eve of the 2nd of September called the Carnival of the Calendar. It's an outdoor festival of music, poetry and dance to celebrate the 11-day leap. Mostly Leaplings attend but a few local Annuals help organise it. It's hidden from the 1752 population but, to be honest, most of them were a bit cross about losing out on the 11 days so the last thing they'd want to do is celebrate.

'It's almost impossible to obtain a ticket and impossible to sneak in. I've only managed to attend twice; maybe I'll never be able to attend again.' Mrs Grayling sighs. 'Leaplings come from all over the timeline so they had the wisdom to severely limit the numbers. Remember, the past is fixed. You can't change it. If a thousand people attended that night, that's what happened.'

Mrs Zhong raises her eyebrows ever so slightly like she disapproves of the Carnival. But I LOVE the sound of it. When I listen to music, I feel like I've gone back in time to the place it was made; poetry's like spells that only work if you say them out loud; and dance is what MC^2 and Kwesi do when they're signing together. Kwesi's an Infinite too who speaks with his hands. I can't imagine Mrs Grayling dancing but I like her a bit more now I've seen her other side. Thinking about that helps me relax. Mrs Zhong continues her talk.

'Leaplings, there are plenty more important historical reasons to visit 1752. Many tourists wish to see their favourite museum artefacts when they were new. We get lots of donations.' She smiles.

'I work with a very specialised time-travel team to authenticate them. Every object has a story; we have to make sure the story is true. And check the objects haven't been stolen. Any questions?'

Several hands go up but I find myself on my feet. I didn't mean to stand up; it's just habit. Mrs C Eckler has been helping me break it. We always had to stand in primary school but we don't in secondary. I sit down, embarrassed. But Mrs Zhong smiles at me.

'You must be Elle. I've read your poem; it's unique. Please ask your question.'

'Do you get lots of stolen goods?'

'Rarely stolen. We get lots of 1752 artefacts that are of no use to us. A time-tourist might purchase a rag doll in 1752 for their child back home in the present but their child rejects it. They donate it to us. The problem is, the item's brand new. It hasn't aged 269 years, so we reject it too. Whereas if someone discovers or inherits an object passed down through generations, my experts check out its history.'

Big Ben is shuffling in his seat. I can tell he's desperate to ask another question. He raises his hand and I'm pleased Mrs Zhong chooses him again.

'Do people steal from the museum?'

'A very good question. Thefts are very rare. Rarer than Leaplings with The Gift! We've only ever had two burglaries, both from this gallery, many, many years ago.'

'What did they steal?' Jake, and he didn't put his hand up. Again!

'Sorry, we're not allowed to disclose the details to the general public.' Mrs Zhong purses her lips like she's stopping the words coming out by mistake. As she says this, I'm aware someone just leapt into the corner of the room. She's tall and tanned with long black hair wound up on her head in an elaborate sculpture of the Eiffel Tower that reminds me of Season, our friend from 2048, but this woman is younger. She could be the same age as Mrs C Eckler, which is 37. Her mid-blue jeans and jacket are made of a shimmering fabric that hasn't been invented yet. I watch closely in case they change colour. She walks into the centre of the room like she owns it and holds out her hand to Mrs Zhong.

'Anno. And you must be Mrs Zhong. Sorry I'm early, something cropped up. I need to speak NOW so I can attend an important meeting.'

Mrs Zhong lowers her eyebrows for a split second. I don't blame her. It's only 9:17 and Anno has interrupted her introduction. Being early is as bad as being late. Then Mrs Zhong smiles with her mouth but not her eyes.

'Please welcome Mrs Anno, Director of Movement, co-founder of the Music, Maths and Movement School, who has come to talk about a recent acquisition in our 1752 collection.'

'Anno will suffice.' She taps her phone like she's timing her speech. 'Anno means year or in the year of in Latin. In addition to my other roles, I'm a sculptor who works with artefacts from leap years.'

I narrow my eyes at her as I start to feel panic surge up inside me. I find sudden changes in plan difficult, especially as my presentation is taking place straight afterwards, where I have to read my poem out loud and take questions from the audience. Now I don't know exactly what time I'll have to stand up. Will it be in five minutes' time at 9:22, which is a messy, in-between number, or will Anno shorten her speech because she has to rush off to her meeting? I was already anxious about the reading but that was manageable. Now, my anxiety has gone into overdrive. Many more possibilities start buzzing round my head until I feel dizzy and overwhelmed.

Mrs C Eckler comes over to me and whispers, 'Do you need time-out?'

I shake my head. I need to remain in the room. If I leave, it will be even more stressful to enter again. I must try to get into the zone. The zone in athletics is when you don't feel like you're making any effort at all, and the world is completely shut out. It's wonderful! I breathe slowly and focus on the first line of my poem:

Is infinity ingrained in 11 missing days?

But at the same time, I can hear Anno begin her talk and I jump when I hear 'Infinity-Glass'. Mrs Zhong has placed a large hour-glass on a small centre table to the right of Anno. I do what-big-eyes; on the museum website there was no photo, just an entry saying: 'Recently acquired, 1752 maritime sandglass with engraved infinity symbols, oak, black sand. To mark the 11 missing days.' That's what I based my poem on. I've always loved the symmetry of an hourglass and I was excited by the infinity symbols, but had no idea it would be so beautiful.

It's the same height as a relay baton and made of dark wood

that's very worn and blackened in places. The bases at each end and the three connecting columns are engraved with infinity signs: ∞ ∞ ∞! The sand inside the glass bulbs is black and grainy and looks like glitter, exactly how I imagined it. As Mrs Zhong turns the hourglass upside down, for a split second, I see the infinity symbol in the shape of the glass, too: ∞. Then it looks like a number 8 as the sand begins to pour through and I focus on Anno's voice.

'Imagine it's 1752. Time changes on your ship when you sail around the earth so you leave your traditional clock at home. Marine sandglasses tell the time on board a ship; accurate mechanical timepieces that can cope with the conditions at sea are yet to be invented.'

Excitement takes over from anxiety. I can't focus on all of Anno's talk but some words come through like '1752' and 'engravings' and 'maritime' which, like marine, means of the sea. I'm staring at the Infinity-Glass with a strong sense of déjà vu: the ∞ symbol is the sign of The Infinites. But I must try to focus on the here and now. Anno's voice has gone lower and slower; her speech will soon end:

'Leaplings, the Infinity-Glass has only recently been donated, anonymously, to this museum. History is a story we are continually rewriting.' She pauses for a split second. 'We don't yet know who made it; or who engraved the infinity signs. In this age of synthetic materials, we can admire this practical sculpture of wood and glass and sand. But we DO know this: the Infinity-Glass was made in 1752, before the 2nd of September. We Leaplings value 1752 artefacts above all others but this one's

13

extra special. It was purchased by Dr Johnson, the famous lexicographer, writer of dictionaries, and given as a present to his young black servant, Francis Barber. It's referred to in a letter Francis wrote years later as "the Glass you bestowed upon me prior to the 11-day leap". History adds value: celebrity multiplies it. The Infinity-Glass is priceless.'

The gallery is quiet like everyone's stopped breathing and all focus is on the Infinity-Glass. Anno nods her head as if taking a bow and I notice Mrs Zhong taking a photo of Anno with her elaborate Eiffel Tower hairstyle standing next to the Infinity-Glass. Mrs C Eckler begins to clap, which means we have to clap too.

Anno waits for it to go quiet again. Then she says, 'Every year, this museum runs a 1752 Poetry Prize. The winner for 2021 is Elle Ifiè from Intercalary International School. We are especially pleased to welcome Elle since she'll be participating in our Music, Maths and Movement Activity Day this Wednesday. Elle, please take the stage to read your poem.' Anno walks to the left-hand side of the room and waits for me to take her place.

I instantly feel sick with over-excitement as Big Ben starts filming on his Chronophone. I remember to take more slow, deep breaths to calm myself down. Somehow, my legs begin to walk to the front of the room.

But before I get there, something happens.

A figure, dressed head to toe in a black catsuit, appears out of thin air, grabs the Infinity-Glass, tilts their head to the right, and disappears. A split second later, an identical figure appears, stares at me, and disappears instantly!

14

It happens so quickly, I stop in my tracks, not sure what to do next. My heart is thumping in my chest like I just ran the 100 metres. Did I imagine it, or did the second figure look me straight in the eye before they disappeared? I couldn't SEE their eyes but I felt their gaze. I stared back. I feel sick. I don't know what to do. I'm tongue-tied. Not from anxiety, from surprise.

Some pupils are shouting, some have left their seats and museum assistants appear out of nowhere, trying to create some kind of order, but everything feels like it's happening behind a glass screen. I can only focus on what just happened.

Someone just stole the Infinity-Glass!

Someone else tried to stop them but they were too late. Or maybe they wanted to steal it for themselves and were too late because it had already been stolen.

Or the first person came back by mistake. Or deliberately. But why?

I don't know what just happened but I know one thing for sure: this is a job for The Infinites!

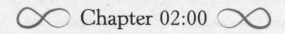

Chapter 02:00

ACTION REPLAY

'If I'm a thief, I'll burglarise the future!' says Big Ben, biting into a ham sandwich.

'Why's that, mate?' says Jake.

'Future inventions are always better.'

It's lunchtime. We're back in school but not IN school. We're sitting on picnic mats in the shade under the trees at the edge of the school playing field. Big Ben, Jake, Maria and I are sharing a large mat. Mrs C Eckler has given us the day off because it's not fair to make us have lessons after ANOTHER school trip has ended in disaster. Even though Big Ben and I aren't boarders, we're not allowed to go home. We have to stay in school until the end of the day.

I open my lunchbox and see Grandma packed the white grapes on top of the flatbread. I try one. It's delicious.

'Does anyone want some grapes?'

'Thanks, Elle,' says Maria, popping one into her mouth before she smiles at Big Ben. 'I like the future too cos it's not fixed like the past. It's exciting and crazy and ANYTHING can happen.'

Jake's shaking his head. 'Is the past REALLY fixed?'

'That's what most Leaplings think, isn't it?' Maria shrugs. 'Time's like a tree: the past is its roots; the present is moving up the trunk of the tree where you have the choice of lots of different branches; and the future's the different branches still growing. That's what I believe.'

'Where's the proof the past is fixed?' says Big Ben. 'You have to have evidence.'

I pick up my flatbread. 'I had a messing-up-history lesson in Sixth Year at my old school. Our teacher said you have to be careful when you leap back in time in case you swat a fly and Hitler ends up winning World War Two.'

Big Ben frowns. 'There's two opposite views. The past is fixed; the past can be changed. Only one is correct or it's not logical. Which one?' He takes a huge bite of his sandwich.

'I think the past can be changed,' says Jake. 'And that your old teacher was right, Elle. When I go back in time, I won't swat a fly, I'll swat Hitler and save lives.'

I do what-big-eyes. It's good Jake wants to save the world but surely he wouldn't take the risk of messing with space–time? Who would?

Maria laughs. 'You won't, Jake. You'll fall over and bang your head before you even find Hitler and have to leap back to 2021 because what happened, happened!'

Big Ben has closed his eyes, like he's solving a maths problem. 'By the law of probabilities, some time in history, a Leapling

17

must have tried to change the past. If they succeeded, they'd be famous in PPF. We don't study it. Therefore they must have failed and the past is fixed.'

'Exactly!' says Maria. 'What do you think, Elle?'

I pause before I answer. I often worry someone like Jake could rupture the space–time continuum by trying to change the past but, like Big Ben said, we don't have any evidence that's ever happened. But how do we know it's NEVER happened? Maybe it has and it was a disaster and they only teach us about it when we're mature enough not to attempt it ourselves. Or someone did it secretly and managed to repair the rupture before they got found out. Maybe it hasn't happened but they want to stop us accidentally leaping too far back in time before humans existed and we get killed by a dinosaur! I find my mouth speaking before my brain's caught up.

'I think the past is fixed. That's why I prefer it.'

Maria smiles. 'It is. Which is why I think the future's more exciting. But futuristic THINGS aren't always better. Old things have character.'

'And sometimes the new things don't work as well,' I say. 'When Bob Beamon did his long jump record, the high-tech measuring instrument fell short. They had to buy an old-fashioned measuring tape to do it correctly.'

Big Ben shakes his head. 'Future inventions are always better. If I'm a thief, I'd steal a prototype from the future and make an eco-supercar.'

A Leapling could steal something from the future to help them create something better in the present but that would be

18

an Anachronism, a crime across the timeline. Anachronisms are illegal.

'I'd never steal,' I say.

'What if you were starving hungry and living on the streets?' says Maria, eating three grapes at a time. I take a big bite from my flatbread.

'That would be different; that would be survival.'

'I'd steal the crown jewels,' says Maria, 'because they're old and priceless.'

'Too girly,' says Jake.

'Not to WEAR!' says Maria. 'Anyway, boys wear jewellery too. I'd sell them to the highest bidder.'

'IF I were a thief, I'd steal something with a history,' I say.

'Like the crown jewels?' says Maria.

'No. It would have to be a story I liked.'

'The Infinity-Glass, then. You wrote a poem about it.'

'I never got to read it.'

'Maybe it was you, Elle. You leapt forward or back in time to steal the Glass so the present Elle could get out of reading.'

'Not logical,' says Big Ben. 'The present Elle isn't Elle at the museum this morning. The present Elle is the one sitting here now and now and now and—'

'You're right, Big Ben,' I say, helping him manage his repetition but still feel appreciated. 'The present is where the past and the future meet.'

∞

19

Big Ben and I are walking round the school grounds. It's hot and humid and I wish it would rain.

'I got it on my Chronophone,' says Big Ben.

Of course! He was filming my reading but got the theft instead.

We sit down in front of the athletics shed. We can still see our friends at the other side of the field but this is private enough. Big Ben takes his big silver Chronophone out of his rucksack. We're allowed to use our mobile phones today because it's a day off. But I can tell he wants this to be secret. He could have shown me the video when the others were there. They know he and I have Chronophones. They think we won them on the 2048 school trip but, of course, they were a present from our fellow Infinite, MC².

Big Ben presses play. I see myself slowly walking down the left-hand aisle to the front of the room and remember how anxious I felt but excited at the same time, my heart almost leaping out of my chest. You can't see my face at all because I have my back to the camera. When I'm halfway there, the picture swerves to the right just in time to catch the first catsuited figure appear out of thin air, grab the Infinity-Glass, tilt their head to the right and disappear; followed by the second figure, who looks at the empty table, looks at ME and disappears instantly. The suits are head to toe, so whoever they are, their hair, face and skin are totally covered.

Then the room erupts into chaos, which I thankfully managed to shut out at the time to prevent sensory overload. After three seconds of that, the video stops.

'I can't believe you got it ALL on film, BB!'

Big Ben smiles. 'I can split-second leap too. Not just you! I felt a rush of air ahead. I moved my phone quick to catch it.'

You need extra-fast reflexes to leap to a nanosecond. Big Ben and I have been practising for months. I kept it a secret at first but you can't keep secrets from your best friend. If they know you well, they find out in the end.

'Did you see them stare at me?'

'What do you mean?'

'The second figure. They stared straight at me. Play it back.'

'I thought they were looking at the empty case. Where they got the Infinity-Glass.'

I hadn't thought of that. I didn't notice where they kept the Infinity-Glass in the first place. It might have been in the archives. Archives are big rooms where they look after objects they don't want the public to see.

'BB,' I say, 'did you take any photos of the gallery?'

'No. The stuff's too old.'

Typical Big Ben. I bet he would have taken loads of photos upstairs. But he wasn't to know we'd need it as evidence. What was the second person looking at? Maybe they WERE checking to see if the Infinity-Glass was in its case or not. We may never know.

'Shouldn't we do something? Try to find it. Or leap back to this morning to stop the theft or—'

'Too dangerous,' Big Ben interrupts me.

He's right. You shouldn't leap to the past until you're 4-leap. It's not illegal but not advisable. My constant anxiety surges: there's that chance you may be too inexperienced and change

21

something in the past by mistake, like tread on a caterpillar and indirectly cause World War Three. But that doesn't stop me wanting to catch the thief and find the Infinity-Glass.

'Can't we look for it in the present?'

'Elle, the two figures are the same size. They might be the same . . .'

Big Ben suddenly becomes transfixed, staring across the field at our classmates. He stands up, sneezes and frowns. I look in the same direction but can't see anything.

A split second later, there's a rush of air, a flicker and two outlines appear in front of us, a boy and a girl, the boy with an afro, the girl with long straggly hair parted in the middle; his hair becomes solid and ginger, hers becomes black; Kwesi and GMT. Our fellow Infinites! But they're 17 and have left school, so why are they here? And where's MC^2? Without him, we're only four out of five.

'L, BB. Bad news!' says GMT and I know it must be serious because she's using our Infinite code names. 'It's MC.' I feel sick. I know what she's going to say before she says it.

'He just got arrested. For stealing the Infinity-Glass!'

Even though I guessed in advance, I'm still shocked, as if her saying it out loud makes it real. Big Ben and I look at each other, our mouths a capital O.

∞ Chapter 03:00 ∞

MC² MINUS THE SQUARED

'Has he confessed? DID he steal it?' I say.

'No to both. MC's no thief!' GMT looks upset. She's always denied MC² ever stole anything, even though he confessed to my class last year that he stole watches in the past to sell in the future and vice versa. MC² gave half that lesson in rap and riddles, which is how he speaks to channel his ADHD. And his hyperactivity's awesome: he can disappear and reappear on the spot!

GMT looks around the field. 'Can we go someplace else to talk?'

'We're not allowed; it's a school day. Anyway, you shouldn't be here. You don't go to this school.'

I didn't mean to say the second bit, it was thinking out loud and probably sounded unkind. Of course, GMT and Kwesi were right to let us know immediately, even if it meant breaking the rules.

Kwesi holds up both hands twice which means 20 minutes. Then I realise GMT must have spoken with Mrs C Eckler and she was kind enough to let them come over because they're our friends and it's a day off. That's what Big Ben was looking at: Kwesi and GMT across the other side of the field before they leapt in front of us. Our next activity starts in 20 minutes' time.

GMT looks at the watch on her left wrist with the blue leather strap, shakes her head and consults the chunky metallic watch on her right wrist, the solar-powered one that looks like it's from the far future. It glints in the sun.

'OK, guys. We got 20 minutes to hatch a plan.' She sounds like MC^2. 'We gotta get him out.'

'We can't help him escape. Then we'd be criminals too and we'd all go to prison and The Infinites would be history.' I fold my arms.

Big Ben agrees. 'We have to prove he's innocent.'

'Does he have an alibi?' I say.

An alibi is proof you were doing something else when the crime was committed.

'Leaplings can't have alibis.' Big Ben reminds us Leaplings can be in more than one place at a time. He gives the example of a man who was queuing in a bank in the PRESENT but leapt from the future to the same bank and robbed it with a stocking over his head! His present version would have been surprised but known that he was going to commit the crime in the future. Big Ben stands up. 'We need evidence.' He looks even taller than usual because the rest of us are sitting on the grass.

'How can we prove he's innocent if we don't know whether he's guilty?' Everyone looks at me then looks away, except GMT.

'Guys, we have to BELIEVE he's innocent and work from there.'

'We filmed the theft.' Big Ben gets the Chronophone out of his rucksack.

Now it's GMT and Kwesi's turn to look surprised. 'So we DO have evidence. Thought you got to the museum AFTER the theft. Your teacher didn't . . .'

She and Kwesi concentrate on the film. They play it back slowly, frame by frame. At the end, they look at each other. They look worried.

'Do you think it's MC²?' I say.

'It looks like TWO people.' She didn't answer my question.

'He could have had an accomplice.' An accomplice is someone who helps to commit a crime.

'Or one person twice.' Everyone looks at Big Ben now. 'They did the theft then leapt back again. But why?'

GMT looks deep in thought, her eyebrows pulled down to her eyes. 'They moved like lightning. Even on slow mode it's too blurred to tell. They look kinda androgynous. Could be anyone.'

Kwesi claps his hands twice to get our attention. He draws ∞ 8 in the air to signify the Infinity-Glass; clasps opposite wrists to show handcuffs; and raises his left fist for solidarity. We must visit MC² and work out a way to set him free.

But how?

∞

It's 4 o'clock and we're standing outside Do-Time, the prison for Leaplings. Like all other Leapling buildings, it's hidden from public view. It's even more private than our school: you can't walk up to it; you have to LEAP to outside the main entrance. I thought it would be a grey building with lots of barbed wire but it's more like a giant white sugar cube. Although it's a prison, the whiteness makes me feel calm.

GMT explains that the building's coated with extra-strong Anti-Leap so the prisoners can't escape. They also make sure visitors can't smuggle anything in to help a breakout. We have to go through all sorts of checks like we're at an airport, and they put our bags into lockers. At least it's much cooler than outside. When they take Big Ben's rucksack, I'm worried he'll have a meltdown because they're quite rude. A meltdown's when autistic people get overwhelmed with emotions and lose control. Big Ben's meltdowns are always physical: his body shakes and he throws chairs. But some autistic people have shutdowns instead, like me. I don't scream or shout, I lose the ability to speak and have to find a quiet space to recover. I used to hide under the table for hours. But Big Ben doesn't have a meltdown here. When I check his face, I see he's counting to a thousand to help himself calm down. He's coping really well. It's important we all get to see MC^2.

We're lucky to be allowed to see him at all. Most visitors have to wait days before they can visit prisoners. But as MC^2 is under 5-leap and doesn't have any family members, we're allowed in. That sounds like they're being kind but they're not; the Leapling system's tough on crime. They SAY innocent until proven guilty but as MC^2 has been in trouble before, he'll be kept in prison until the trial. If he's found guilty, he'll stay in Do-Time for years!

We only have half an hour to see him and some of that has been taken up with walking down long white corridors with a prison warden with lots of keys jangling from his back pocket. The Young Offenders Wing is the furthest away from the entrance.

MC^2 is sitting on a chair in a square white room with a square window with bars on it that he can talk through. We have to sit in the adjoining room so we can't help him escape. The prison warden sits on a chair in our room; it must be very uncomfortable sitting on so many keys! MC^2 looks exhausted. His antennae dreads have drooped, he's wearing a beige overall instead of his usual graffiti tracksuit and he barely looks up as we come in. When Kwesi raises his left fist to the bars, his infinity tattoo in full view, MC^2 raises his in slow motion. I have a flashback of the moment we rescued Kwesi from the Time Squad Centre in 2100. Now their roles are reversed.

GMT's having trouble remaining seated. 'MC. We'll get you outta this place.'

MC^2 shrugs and looks down at the floor. I feel sad for him and shocked. I've never seen him like this before. I'm not sure whether he's tongue-tied like I get when I'm so upset I CAN'T talk or if he's refusing to talk because he's guilty.

Kwesi draws in the air: ∞ 8. MC^2 shakes his head. GMT's pacing.

'MC, we know you're innocent.'

We don't know he's innocent, but I don't say anything because

I don't want GMT to be angry if I contradict her, or MC² to get sad or angry that I think he's guilty. I find it hard seeing MC² so quiet, like someone sucked all his energy away. Then I have a brainwave.

'Maybe he wants 1-2-1? All of us at once is too much.'

That's how I feel when I'm stressed and need to shut down. It overwhelms me and makes it worse when too many people try to help. MC² has ADHD, he's not autistic, but when his brain focuses on too many things at the same time, he gets overwhelmed too. Plus, it must have been scary being arrested, whether he was guilty or not. No wonder he's exhausted. I look at MC². I THINK he nods. Kwesi starts signing again and the three of us move to the back of the room and face the wall to give them privacy. GMT checks her metallic watch.

'Each of us got five minutes max,' she says.

She still can't keep still; I wish I could do running round the track right now to feel calm but I can't desert my friends.

'If he tells us where the Infinity-Glass is, we could take it back to the museum and they might let him out,' I say.

'Honeybee, he doesn't know where it is.'

'He might tell Kwesi.'

We can't help looking over our shoulders to see Kwesi signing and MC² signing back with jerky movements, like he's angry. I quickly turn my head back to face the wall. It doesn't look good. If he's arguing with his best friend, he's not going to communicate with the rest of us.

When Kwesi's five minutes are up, he walks back to the wall shaking his head, frowning like an old man. GMT's next. I try not to listen in because it's meant to be private but I can't help but hear. GMT's talking too much and too quickly. Maybe she does that when she's upset. The problem is, even if MC^2 wanted to respond, he wouldn't have a chance. Not surprisingly, she comes back shaking her head too. Then it's Big Ben's turn. I'm curious what he'll say. He often thinks in numbers rather than words.

'Do you want to speak with your hands?'

Big Ben knows what it's like when you can't use verbal language so he's trying to give MC^2 another way to communicate. ADHD's different to autism, though some people have both. MC^2 usually talks or body blinks too much. But he obviously doesn't want to try speaking with his hands because Big Ben speaks again.

'Do you want to speak in numbers?'

Silence again. Then a very low mumble even I can't hear. What did he say? Big Ben bounds across the room, his legs looking longer than ever.

'1752,' he says.

'That's a whole year!' I say. 'We don't know the date or place or anything.'

I look back at MC^2. He's looking at Kwesi and Kwesi shakes his head vigorously. Something's going on. Maybe 1752 is a better clue than I thought and that's what they were arguing about.

Now it's my turn. I sit on the chair and turn my head to focus on the left of the window so I'm not staring straight at MC^2 and he's not staring straight at me. I take a deep breath like I'm about to push out of the blocks for the 100 metres.

'What does 1752 MEAN?'

I look at him out of the corner of my eyes and he blinks several times like the old MC^2. That makes me happy but I hope he's not going to burst into a rap. It would be impossible to remember the words and we need all the clues we can get.

'France is 1752,' he says, in a voice that sounds like it's underwater.

Then his eyes go blank again and I know he's not going to speak any more. It wouldn't be fair to try to make him. I go back to the group.

'He said France is 1752. Does it mean we have to go to France?'

GMT and Kwesi shrug their shoulders; the prison warden clears his throat. It's time to leave. When we say goodbye to MC^2 in turns, he looks sad. I hold up my hand to wave at him. He holds up his hand and points at me and Big Ben. I frown but Big Ben's smiling.

'He wants you and me to solve it.'

'Are you sure he means that? And why us? Kwesi and GMT are closer to him and older and—'

'He pointed at us. This is our second assignment. And we'll be Level 2.'

'I don't want to go to France. I want to see the Eiffel Tower but not yet.'

We're walking back down the corridor. Kwesi seems happier now. GMT's more relaxed to have a corridor to walk down rather than being stuck in a room, but she's not happy. It must have been difficult that MC^2 didn't speak to her.

When we've collected our bags, Kwesi takes out his

Chronophone and makes us all do the same. He taps into it so fast I can barely see his fingers. A split second later, all our phones buzz. I look at my screen. Kwesi's sent us a message:

Got to work. Meet again soon. Don't do nothing without me.

We touch fists with him and he disappears into thin air.

I check my watch: 16:40. I need to go home. Grandma will be back from her cleaning job by 17:30 and I have to cook beans for dinner. They've been soaked and boiled but they need time to absorb the stew. Big Ben needs to go home too. But GMT's in no hurry to get back to the late 1960s.

'You guys wanna hang out?'

'We can't. I have to cook and Big Ben has to go home or his mum will worry.'

'OK, honeybee. But we need to meet later. Things just got tricky. It's Kwesi and MC; I saw what they were signing. We gotta discuss that and—'

'Can't you tell us now?'

'Too complicated. Can we meet at your flat, Elle? You, me and Big Ben. Didn't you say your Grandma's out tonight?'

'Yes, she has her extra cleaning job. But Kwesi texted don't do nothing without me. It's not fair to meet up behind his back.'

'I know. But you haven't heard what they were signing.'

She's right. We don't know what Kwesi or MC² signed to each other but we know what he said: France is 1752.

If we work out what that means, we might be able to set him free.

∞ Chapter 04:00 ∞

CONFESSION OF A CAT BURGLAR

When GMT knocks on the outside door at exactly 8 o'clock and I go down the stairs to let her in, Grandma shouts from our flat loud enough for all the other occupants of The Mush-Rooms to hear.

'GT, you are welcome! I am very pleased with you.'

She means pleased to see you and she always gets GMT's name wrong. She smiles as we walk into the flat and turns on the fan which makes a whirring noise. I don't know which is worse, excess heat or the irritating noise. GMT's wearing a velvet kaftan which is a long, loose tunic covered in swirly patterns in purple and blue and she's carrying a matching purple holdall. I love the way she dresses but if I wore clothes like that, everyone would stare at me and I'd be embarrassed, even if I looked good. When people stare at me, I FEEL them looking, like their eyes are laser beams.

GMT's only been round a couple of times since the leap

birthday party but Grandma always remembers she's vegetarian and offers her whatever we have on the stove. Tonight, it's black-eyed beans cooked in a stew made of tomatoes, onions and scotch bonnet peppers with boiled green plantain. I ate mine with Grandma earlier, concentrating on the damp patch on the wall so I didn't get overwhelmed by the different colours, but I enjoyed the food. Now, Grandma watches GMT eating, fixates on the swirly patterns on her sleeve.

'You dress very well. Please, I beg, take Elle to the boutique. She needs new clothes. Look her trouser in dispute with her trainer. And she refuses to wear brassiere!'

Grandma's right. I HAVE grown a lot the past few months. I DO need new clothes, and I want to try different colours, not just white, but I'm not quite ready. I wish Grandma would get over her obsession with bras. I don't need one. GMT knows this and smiles.

'Ma'am, it sure is the longest day but the shops are closed now. Elle and I just wanna hang out. I mean, chat.'

'That is good. Elle needs more talk, less running. Don't chat till midnight or you'll turn into a toad.'

Grandma gets her stories muddled up but she's smiling so this time it must be a joke. She's about to say something else when we hear more knocking outside. Big Ben! Grandma goes into the bedroom to change into fresh clothes while I answer the door.

∞

33

'So what were they signing?' I stare into the white tablecloth and try not to focus on the stains.

'MC wants you and Big Ben to take on the case, starting with leaping back to the crime scene this morning; Kwesi says no.'

Big Ben pauses several seconds. 'I want to be Level 2.'

'I don't want to go to France,' I say. 'Not without a grown-up. It's even more dangerous than going back in time to the museum this morning to stop the theft. You said it was too dangerous yourself!'

Big Ben nods. 'It WAS. But the odds changed. Now MC² is arrested.'

'He's right, honeybee.' GMT gets up from her chair and starts pacing. 'I'm with MC on this one. He's the one behind bars. And it has to be you and Big Ben. Kwesi's working now; he doesn't have the time.'

'What about you? You just hang out at festivals and you don't go to school so you've got the most time!'

I walk over to the tap and pour everyone a glass of water. I don't want to look at GMT in case she's cross. I'm worried I sounded rude.

'It's complicated,' she says.

'You said that before. Are you worried Kwesi will be angry we met up without him?'

'Yeah. Kwesi's clever. I wonder why he doesn't want you to leap? Something doesn't add up. I guess he thinks you and Big Ben could get into trouble if anyone finds out you leaped back in time. You're only 3-leap +1.'

'It's not illegal,' says Big Ben.

GMT faces us. 'BB's right. You just need to leap back to this morning and—'

'Stop the theft.' I finish her sentence for her. 'But how can we do that if the past is fixed?'

'It is,' says GMT. 'You can't STOP the theft cos it already happened. But you can try to get the Glass back.'

'What do you mean?'

'The past IS fixed. The thief stole the Glass; someone witnessed the theft then leapt back in time to get the Glass back. Probably you, Elle.' She sits back down and takes a long swig of her water.

I frown just thinking about it. Then I'm reminded of Maria's tree: the past being the fixed roots. My anxiety is making me worry about messing with space–time. 'So if I leap back in time to TRY to stop the theft, that's what actually happened.'

Big Ben's smiling. 'Logical.'

'You got it, Elle; it's up to you. You gotta leap back to the museum then leap after the thief. Big Ben should be on standby in case of problems.'

'What if MC^2 was the second person, trying to stop the theft, and failed and feels ashamed and that's why he's not speaking?'

Big Ben's shaking his head vigorously. 'What if it's the same person?'

'Why would the thief come back?' GMT pauses. 'No. I think there were two people. Speaking of . . .'

She unzips her purple swirly holdall and pulls out what looks like a black tracksuit. But when she separates it, I realise it's not a top and a bottom: it's two black all-in-ones. Cat burglar outfits!

She lays them on the table; they look odd, like shedded human skins on the white background, and I shudder. Big Ben looks at me and raises his eyebrows. I wonder if he's thinking what I'm thinking. GMT reads our minds.

'You'll both have to wear these for the mission. The best skinsuits not yet invented. "Total disguise, even the eyes", says the advert, but you can breathe real good.'

I say, 'I can't wear tight clothes!'

and Big Ben says, 'Not logical. It won't fit.'

at exactly the same time.

GMT wipes her brow. 'Guys, Elle can't do this alone. Too dangerous. Big Ben's gotta be on standby but he still has to be in disguise.' She holds up one of the catsuits. 'It'll stretch.'

'There's stretch and stre-e-e-e-e-e-tch!' I say. 'And I've got a better idea: you wear it, GMT. It'll fit YOU. You can come on standby and—'

'NO!'

Something's wrong. GMT doesn't look like chilled-out GMT any more. She looks scared. Surely she can't be scared of leaping; she leaps all over the timeline! Big Ben and I get up from our chairs. If GMT's having a meltdown, she needs space. She doesn't want the sensory overload of TWO of us trying to help. But she makes a movement with her hands; she wants us to stay in our seats. When she speaks, she sounds like she's squeezing each word out, one by one.

'Guys. I . . . can't . . .'

'Why not? Do you hate tight clothes, too?' I say. 'And where did you get them, the cat burglar shop?'

36

'No. I guess . . . it's time you knew.'

'Knew what?' we say, together.

There's a very long pause. 'MC never stole nothing. It was me!'

'You stole the Infinity-Glass?' My mouth is a capital O.

'No. The watches, in the past and the future. It was me who stole the watches; MC only sold them.'

And suddenly it all makes sense. That's why GMT was so sure MC wasn't a thief. Because it was HER all along. And these must be the outfits they wore as partners in crime. I look at her through narrowed eyes.

'You let MC² take the blame when it was you! How can you say he's your friend?'

'Elle, we were in it together. We swore if we ever got caught, he'd take the blame. Better one of us locked away than two. When he got the Time Squad job instead of Young Offenders—'

'You're a thief! And you lied to the police. How do we know you didn't steal this morning? Why should we trust you now?'

'Elle, I ain't worn the suit since. How could I?'

'I don't want a criminal in this flat. Leave now.'

GMT opens her mouth then shuts it again. The silence is what she doesn't say and I feel very uncomfortable. When she grabs her holdall, I notice her hands are shaking. She takes a few deep breaths and disappears, her jagged outline taking a few seconds to fade.

Big Ben says nothing. He knows I need time to process. I'm overwhelmed with emotions, angry but sad and scared at the same time. I like GMT, she's like a big sister, but suddenly she's not the person I thought she was. And I'm scared for MC^2: if he's found guilty, they'll be extra harsh on him.

I look at Big Ben. I know he's thinking what I'm thinking. We don't need words. It will be uncomfortable and dangerous but I have no choice.

I must leap back to this morning.

I must try to catch the thief.

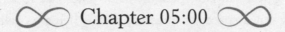

Chapter 05:00

THE LEAPING
LAMBORGHINI

It's 9 p.m., the sun's dipping behind the trees and daylight's beginning to fade. Big Ben and I leapt to the start of the school drive so I didn't have to walk through town looking like a cat burglar with a rucksack. He's in normal clothes. I wanted to leap straight to the long-jump pit, my favourite place in the world, so I could warm up before the real thing but Big Ben says it's better to walk up here first, like it's a school day. He's right. I'm still upset from GMT's confession and the tree-lined drive always calms me. It's so relaxing in the half light I don't even have the urge to run.

We've only been walking a minute when we hear a strange noise from the sky, like a near-silent plane. I hear it seconds before I see the headlights, two massive burning eyes. It's not a plane; it's a car! And a flying car means only one thing: Season. Season in her eco-friendly supercar, Ferrari Forever. What's she doing here?

Big Ben does running up and down, whooping and flapping his hands as he always does when he sees a particularly cool car. His flapping is a stim; he's stimming because he's super happy! Stims are repetitive movements like spinning or sounds like humming that autistic people make when we're excited, or checking out a space, or stressed, and it helps us calm down. Sometimes our emotions are so intense, we have to do something with the energy to think more clearly.

I continue walking up the left-hand side of the drive but my heart's thumping in my chest. The car begins to descend; the wingflaps open until it lands about 200 metres in front of us, slowly coming into view. Big Ben stops running and I stop with him at the side of the road.

'Good landing,' he says.

The car stops, too, and I get the odd impression the car itself is looking at us through its headlights. I shiver. It's red, not lime-green, as I expected. Big Ben squints.

'Elle,' he says, 'it's not a Ferrari, it's a—'

There's a whirring noise and the car begins to accelerate. It's coming down the drive full throttle on the WRONG side of the road. Oh my Chrono, it's coming directly at US! It takes two or three seconds for this to sink in, just enough time for us to throw ourselves into the trees like the Fosbury Flop as the car careers off the road, then back onto the tarmac and takes off into the air!

Big Ben's the first to stand up. He comes over and kneels down beside me.

There's a long pause. 'Elle?' he says.

I nod my head. I don't want to speak or move at all but I want

40

him to know I'm OK. I don't want him to worry about me. He slowly holds out his hand but I shake my head and he understands. After what seems like an hour but is actually five minutes, I try to stand up but I'm too dizzy. I'm shaken and bruised but at least nothing's broken. It could have been a whole lot worse. We could be dead! I need to stay seated a bit longer but can see Big Ben's impatient to leave because he's upright now, bending his knees like he's limbering up for a sprint.

'They tried to stop us leaping.'

'How did they know we were going to?' I rub my left shoulder to stop it throbbing.

'The theft happened this morning. They had time to work it out.'

'But how did they know we're here?'

'Don't know.' Big Ben's rubbing his left knee. 'It was a Lamborghini.'

'Did you see the number plate?'

'No, but it might be a clue. Elle,' he raises his eyes to the sky, 'we need to go. They could come back!'

That makes me stand up immediately. Dizzy or not, there's no time to lose!

∞

No time for a warm-up. No time to enjoy my favourite place in the whole world.

I stand on the runway at the long-jump pit to psych myself up.

I visualise the 1752 Gallery, the exact spot where the second figure appeared.

I focus on the date: the 21st of June 2021.

I focus on the time: 9:21.22.

I close my eyes. And I leap!

Just before I arrive, I feel it. Something hard bashes my chest. I open my eyes and see a figure in a catsuit holding the Infinity-Glass. I fully arrive. In a split second, I see myself, in my white tunic and trousers, frozen in the aisle; the figure disappears from sight; I grab the outline of the Glass!

So far so good. What happened, happened. But now, I have to wrestle the Infinity-Glass away from the thief. Is it MC^2 or someone else? Whoever they are, they're strong. But I have an advantage; they weren't expecting a fight and I'm VERY strong from athletics training, with super-quick reflexes. All my strength training comes into play. All the press-ups and punch-bags and precision leaping. We're wrestling in time's dark tunnel, tiny white numbers colliding with our faces like hail.

And I can feel the thief weakening, while I could keep this going for five minutes. I take my opportunity and give the Glass an extra fierce tug and it's in my hands. I focus on the school long-jump pit, 9:30 in the EVENING, the 21st of June 2021 and squeeze my eyes shut. But something weird happens, a leap-clash, the two of us collide and I lose focus for a second. There's a blow to my head and I fall, still clinging to the Glass. Whatever happens, I can't let go of it, I can't let The Infinites down. My body goes fizzy and I'm seeing two lots of digits at the same time, fuzzy white on black, 15:00, 16:00, hours going forward in time to the evening, and bolder and brighter, 12:00, 11:00, hours going back in time to the morning. I feel dizzy, intense nausea sweeps over me and I close my eyes completely. Then, there's total blackness and everything goes still.

∞

When I open my eyes, I'm sitting in the middle of a small oak-panelled room, still clinging to the Glass! I gaze down at it. The grains of black sand pour through the join like liquid, the infinity engravings reminding me of the symbols MC^2 carved into a tree in 2048. The Infinity-Glass is oak, too, though not as well preserved. It matches these surroundings, it belongs here. These rooms must have been designed in the 1700s. But I mustn't get side-tracked; I have a job to do.

I must leap back to the long-jump pit. I concentrate; I close my eyes but I feel like an uncharged battery. Maybe that's what MC^2 felt like. Leaping isn't going to work right now. I put the Infinity-Glass on the floor beside me. I don't know where I am or WHEN I am and have no means of escape. But I can't give up now, I'm a Level 1 Infinite. I need to check my phone; that will give me a location.

And I must text Big Ben. I must have swapped places with the thief when we leap-clashed; we've landed in each other's destination. That means the thief's at the long-jump pit. They might attack Big Ben or, worse, when Big Ben realises they're not me, he might think they've hurt me and attack THEM. I take the rucksack off my back, which aches a bit after the wrestling and jumping to avoid being run over. I'm just unzipping the front section which holds my Chronophone, fingers numb from holding the Glass so tightly, when a door creaks open and a slimy-looking man pokes his head around it like a tortoise peeping out of its shell.

∞ Chapter 06:00 ∞

THE VICIOUS CIRCLE

He has bronze skin, blue eyes and black hair as shiny as gloss paint. A second later, his body follows. He's tall and square, wearing a long purple hooded gown.

'A most profitable morning!' he says, rubbing his hands together. 'A lucrative leap! The Vicious Circle are expecting you.'

My heart thumps in my chest. He thinks I'm the thief; we look identical in our catsuit disguises. I open my mouth to correct him, but if I do, I'll be in serious danger and not be able to leap away. Whereas if I say nothing and do as he says, I might be able to find some clues. His face creases into an oily smile.

'Follow me,' he says, 'And don't forget to bring the prize!'

I throw my rucksack onto my back, lift the Infinity-Glass, surprised by how heavy it is, and follow him into a round, dark, oak-panelled room with no windows that smells of the woods after it's rained. I do big-eyes behind my mask: I've been here before. I came with Grandma to swear the Oath of Secrecy. This time, though, there's a large round table in the

45

middle of the room and people sitting at it, wearing purple-hooded clothing, eight of them. Four of the chairs are empty and I realise there are 12 in total, arranged like a clock. Some of the people stare at me and I feel uncomfortable; then I realise they're not looking at me at all, they're looking at the Infinity-Glass.

It gives me a chance to check out the clock-inspired circle. Where numbers 1 and 2 would be, two black teenage boys gaze, mesmerised. They're wearing purple hoodies, 1 with his hood up, 2 showing intricate patterns like a maze carved into his hair. 3 is empty and 4's a man with light-brown skin and a long narrow face. I can't see 5, 6 or 7 because they have their backs to me and their hoods up. 8's empty. In 9 is a squat woman with short jet-black hair, fierce as a shot putter; in 10, an old woman like a future version of Mrs Zhong, who looks like she'd kneel down on the ground and worship the Infinity-Glass if she wasn't so ancient. 11 and 12 are also empty.

My oily-haired host takes the seat at 3, next to the teens, but tells me to remain standing with the Glass. The clock on the wall says 9:30 but I know it must be morning not evening. It's not long after the theft took place. The squat black-haired woman shuffles in her seat.

'The Double M's late!' She laughs and laughs but her mouth is a minus sign.

I gasp aloud; the Double M is Millennia, the criminal mastermind, my arch enemy! This must be her inner circle. I'm in much more danger than I ever imagined. I take slow, deep breaths to stop my heart leaping out of my chest. Thankfully, the squat woman's laughter is loud. No one heard me. The teens smile like they're enjoying the joke but Mr Oily Hair frowns.

'Show some respect, Nine,' he says across the circle. 'You're letting down the family.'

'As you pretend to, Three?' It's the old woman who says this, her voice like a car skidding on gravel.

'Oh Meridian, I show OODLES of it.'

'To her face, you do, to advance your position in the Circle. The Three who wishes he were a Twelve. You have much to learn. Your time will come, if you deserve it. As for you,' Meridian looks at Nine, 'do not overestimate your position.'

Nine narrows her eyes. 'Our leader is late. Our leader's too old to leap.' She pauses. 'A late leader's a late leader.'

'You are suggesting Millennia is no longer fit to lead?'

'I am. She weakens with every leap. She should gracefully exit the Circle before she's forcibly exited.'

'Is that a threat?' Meridian fixes her neighbour with her black eyes.

'I could exit the Double M myself but I hold back. Why waste days, weeks, months gathering evidence to convince you when Time will do a better job? She won't last the year. Millennia is past tense.'

'You dare to mock the past? You place yourself above her – whom we hold in such high esteem? Only I, Meridian, can exit Millennia. Not you, nor your family—'

There's a sudden movement at the oak panelling behind Meridian. Everyone stands. We detect the outline of a tall stooped woman in a long hooded robe and a small man in a

47

suit and top hat! The outline becomes solid: Millennia, her short white hair matted against her head, her face ashen, supported by a strange little man in old-fashioned dress with pallid white skin and slate-grey eyes. Maybe it's her husband. The two of them move slowly, unsteadily, like they've just learnt to walk or are 100 years old. I'm reminded of Grandma when her leg is paining her. Mr Oily Hair rushes to pull out the number 12 chair. The weird man leads Millennia over and virtually drops her into it. She slumps forward on the table, her eyes closed. I wonder if she's dead! He stands behind his seat at number 11.

'You may be seated,' he says in a voice high and deep at the same time.

Everyone sits except me. I narrow my eyes at him. Something's not right. His clothes are a man's, he moved slowly and he spoke formally like an adult but his voice is a teen's and his face is smooth. He can't be more than 3-leap! Yet the adults have taken an order from him; even Evil Nine looks impressed. The ancient-infant puffs out his chest.

'Chrono of crime, thieves of time, let us commence!'

On the word commence Millennia opens her eyes. She sits upright and runs her fingers through her damp hair till it looks like an electric shock. Colour floods back into her face. The ancient-infant looks at Millennia for ten full seconds before he slowly takes his seat. When he's fully seated, Millennia speaks.

'Grandfather, we commence.'

My eyes widen under my mask. How can this boy be Millennia's grandfather? But then I focus on Millennia. She

48

stands tall and gazes round the circle till her eyes fix on the Infinity-Glass.

'What, in the name of Time, is that?'

Mr Oily Hair, aka Three, stands up.

'The artefact we informed you of in the previous meeting, esteemed Millennia. The priceless Infinity-Glass that will make ALL our fortunes.' He clears his throat. 'Though, of course, as I myself orchestrated the TIMING of this theft and have provided a safe place to hide it and the thief—'

'Sit down, Three. Whoever took the risk will receive the usual bonus IF we choose to sell it.' Millennia turns to me. 'Who is this?'

'Family,' says Mr Oily Hair, giving me his greasy smile. Millennia nods gravely and addresses me directly.

'Bring it here. Say nothing. I do not wish to hear your voice; I do not wish to know who you are. None of this is happening, do you understand?'

I nod. Millennia's up to her old tricks, pretending she knows nothing about crime or criminals. It IS happening but not in the way she sees it. I'm double-double crossing the Double M. I'm not the criminal she thinks I am AND by nodding, I'm lying. I HATE lying; I purse my lips together so tight they hurt, to stop myself shouting out the truth. I have to. I'm a Level 1 Infinite and this is a Level 2 job.

All eyes are on me. My face burns underneath the disguise as I walk round the right-hand side of the table. I hate people looking at me directly too, but the mask helps a lot and it's easier walking past Mr Oily Hair and the teenage boys than walking past Evil Nine, Meridian and The Grandfather. The circle gets badder the higher up you go.

I place the Infinity-Glass on the table in front of Millennia and remain standing next to her, waiting for instructions. But it's as if she's forgotten I'm still here. She lifts the Glass, her fingers knotted and spotted with age, tracing the indented infinity signs. Then she upturns it, places it on the table and the sand begins to flow.

'Execute it!' she says, turning her face away.

'NO!' Meridian stands up, her hands shaking. 'No.'

'If esteemed Millennia says execute it, that can be easily arranged,' begins Mr Oily Hair, who has also left his seat, 'if by execute, esteemed Millennia is referring to the profitable conclusion of this crime: selling the Glass to the highest bidder on the black market for millions of pounds that will benefit the full Circle for decades. Whereas, if execute were to mean destroy—'

'I indeed mean destroy. The priceless 1752 Infinity-Glass!' Millennia appears to be announcing it but her voice is cold as flint. 'I like "priceless": I'm a businesswoman, I know what this is worth and Dr Johnson's fame triples its price tag. But I already have money. And I like "1752": the perfect holiday destination where Leapers link hands with Annuals and let the calendar do the hard work. How I have profited from 1752. There is much to like. And the 18th century is my favourite of them all. But seeing the Infinity-Glass in the flesh, in the here and now, presents me with a problem.' She pauses. 'Would anyone like to guess what the problem is?'

I almost put up my hand. But this isn't school or the Time Squad Centre in 2048. This is The Vicious Circle. I look around it, at its range of faces, old and young, black and white, and the one empty chair at 8. I wonder who isn't here. Then I look at Meridian, aged and angry, and realise she's the only person old enough and bold enough to stand up to Millennia.

'The problem is, esteemed leader, the infinity symbol.' Meridian pauses. 'You give your enemies too much credit. INFINITY did not commission this hourglass; it is of its time.'

Millennia winces at the word Infinity. Infinity, the wisest bissextile ever, who's leapt to the edge of time but no one's ever seen. Infinity, who supports The Infinites in secret. I can see why Millennia's afraid.

'Meridian, I know very well Infinity did not pay to have an hourglass created in her honour. When Dr Johnson bestowed it upon his favourite servant it was a classical marine timepiece: at some point on the timeline someone added these symbols to taunt me, to humiliate me, to keep me awake at night. Infinity is too powerful, a threat to the very existence of The Vicious Circle. Do you not understand my repulsion?'

'I do. But I do not understand why you wish to DESTROY an invaluable historic Leapling artefact merely because it reminds you of your nemesis.'

'My enemies are more numerous than Infinity. There are others who wish to thwart us. That girl—'

'Elle?'

'A glitch on my timeline.'

'You fear youth?' Meridian raises her eyebrows.

'She is extraordinarily talented. I saw it when she swore the Oath and I have seen it since. But she cannot be working alone.'

'Leader, *tempus fugit*. And time flies even faster in English. You have stated your case and your case is flawed. Out of sight is out of mind. Let us remove it, sell it and enjoy the profit. What is the fate of the Infinity-Glass? Is it to be destroyed or preserved?'

'I stand firm in my conviction,' says Millennia. 'Therefore, we will follow the ancient protocol. As happens in a clash of Elders, The Vicious Circle must take a vote. In preparation . . .'

As Millennia explains the system, I hold the side of the table to stop myself from shaking. I was OK until I heard my own name. But now I'm struggling. There's too much to process and I'm in terrible danger. If only I could crawl under the table and decompress. The only thing saving me is my lack of status. Here, in this disguise and outside The Vicious Circle, I'm invisible. No one cares who I am. And yet I'm Elle, and Millennia hates and fears me almost as much as she hates and fears Infinity.

I continue taking deep breaths and focus back on Millennia announcing the vote.

'Those who wish to destroy the Infinity-Glass, raise their hands.'

Millennia and The Grandfather raise their hands and look round the circle. After several long, uncomfortable seconds, Mr Oily Hair raises his hand half-mast and Seven follows.

'Four members for destruction,' says Millennia. She pauses. 'Those who wish to preserve it for profit?'

Meridian, Evil Nine and both teens raise their hands.

'Four members for preservation.' Millennia gives the teens the cat's eye; she can barely get her words out. 'And those too cowardly to commit to one side or the other and who wish to abstain?'

The remaining three people raise their hands.

Millennia goes into loudspeaker mode. 'It appears the conflict is evenly balanced, four against four. On such occasions, we must resort to the full Circle. We have one missing member, Eight. Eight must cast their vote by Chronophone.'

Everyone takes out their phones, placing them on the table. Millennia fumbles in her robe and produces a purple phone. She taps into it. Everyone's looking at their screens, avoiding Millennia's eye. A few seconds later, her face tightens like a fist.

'It appears,' she says, 'The Vicious Circle have voted five against four to preserve this offensive artefact. Remove it from my sight IMMEDIATELY. And,' looking at me, 'all evidence of this episode.'

Mr Oily Hair quickly steps forward. 'We will find the best buyer for this artefact, esteemed Millennia. My sister can—'

'I know what your sister can do. The case of this INFINITY-Glass is closed. However, I would pay a small fortune to have a glimpse of this same hourglass BEFORE someone saw fit to deface it with infinity symbols. The association of Dr Johnson and 1752 pleases me beyond measure. Of course, we will not be able to sell it; once I have SEEN it, it must be returned to the time and place it was taken. But see it I must. Who will do the job?'

'How much?'

'Enough to make it worth the risk.'

Mr Oily Hair rubs his hands together. 'It is a complex crime as we don't know the exact date the engravings were made. But I'm prepared to arrange it.'

Meridian shakes her head. 'Leader, you go too far. Are you suggesting one of our circle steals and transports a precious glass object from the 18th century to the present day? If it breaks mid-leap, the current aged artefact would not exist for us to sell. You would risk jeopardising both our profit and every single historical event relating to the Glass. The consequences would be catastrophic.'

'Meridian, you know as well as I that Leapers have leapt back in time to attempt to change the past but failed. Maybe one day someone will succeed.' Millennia pauses for three long seconds. 'In the meantime, we might WISH to alter events on our timelines but the past is fixed. There can be no alternative timeline, no other chain of events from the ones that have already taken place. Furthermore, if a body-blinking boy can transport watches, The Vicious Circle can transport an hourglass and return it from whence it came.'

Meridian purses her lips. Mr Oily Hair clears his throat.

'Esteemed Millennia, your wish is—'

Millennia raises her hands flat like she's pushing a heavy object. Mr Oily Hair bows so low, it looks like he's stretching his hamstrings. He lifts the Glass from the table and pushes what I thought was an oak panel directly behind Millennia. It's a door! Only then do I notice there are identical panels behind every seat. There must be 12 antechambers leading off this room. He motions me to follow. I gladly obey.

54

If I'd stayed any longer in that room, I'd DEFINITELY have given myself away by going down on my hands and knees and crawling under the table. But now I'm in the antechamber, out of danger, part of me wants to hit him on the head, wrestle the Infinity-Glass out of his grasp and leap, but he'd be too strong. Even if I took him by surprise, I wouldn't be able to leap away in time. In fact, I might not be able to leap at all. No. I have to continue playing along. He gives me another oily smile.

'You did well. You'll be amply rewarded. Now disappear!'

Oh my Chrono, I have to leap now! Have I got my strength back? I concentrate on the long-jump pit but what time shall I leap back to? Should I stick to my original plan of 9:30 in the evening? I don't want to leap back too early in case I mess with space–time or, worse, collide with myself. And what about the thief? They might be trying to leap here at the same time. I close my eyes, focus on the pit and 9:30 p.m. Luckily, my strength HAS come back. The familiar fizzy feeling takes over my body; I take a few deep breaths and feel the beginnings of a delicate breeze on my face before I open my eyes.

∞

Big Ben is sitting on the grass in front of me.

'Elle?' he says.

I un-velcro the headpiece, shocked how damp my face is underneath.

'I got the Glass but . . .'

55

I have to sit down, suddenly overcome with everything that's happened, and can't finish the sentence. Admitting I had to deliver it into enemy hands is like experiencing it twice. Big Ben shuffles forward on his bottom and puts his arms round me tightly, how I like it. Then he gives me space.

'Is it in your bag?'

I shake my head.

'It's OK,' he says. 'I want you to be OK.'

We sit for a few minutes on the grass, saying nothing at all. Big Ben's the only person I can be silent with and feel comfortable. He doesn't keep talking to try to calm me down. He knows when I need time-out. But he also knows we could still be in danger so we can't stay here too long.

'The thief leapt here,' he says. 'I thought it was you but they ran away from me. You never run away. They didn't run very fast, though.'

I smile. They must have been as tired as I was after we wrestled then collided mid-leap. Like me, they didn't have the strength to leap back straight away. It takes it out of you.

'Where did they go?' I've got my voice back.

'Don't know.'

'They didn't leap back to The Vicious Circle. I would have seen them.'

And then I tell Big Ben everything that happened, from the wrestling in the tunnel of time to the final vote. I can see he's impressed.

'The thief didn't leap back to the Circle this morning in case they met you?'

'No, BB. They were scared they'd get exited for losing the Glass.'

'Exited?'

'I think it means kicked out of The Vicious Circle. But when they say exit, it sounds really scary, like kill,' I say. 'Nine wants to exit Millennia. Meridian says only SHE has the right to do it. They all hate each other.'

'But they sent the Lamborghini to kill US.'

I'd forgotten about that. So much has happened this evening.

'The thief must have said something. How would they know to find us on the school drive this evening?' I stand up. 'BB, I'm scared.'

'No,' says Big Ben. 'You're brave, not scared.'

Big Ben's kind but I AM scared. I want all The Vicious Circle to be arrested and locked up in jail but we have no proof. It would be my word against theirs and then I'd be in even more danger. Anyway, I delivered the stolen Infinity-Glass straight into their hands. They could accuse me of that and I'd be the one in prison!

On top of those thoughts, too many questions are colliding in my head.

Who tried to kill us to stop us leaping?

Who's the thief?

And who's the mystery number Eight who voted to preserve the Infinity-Glass?

∞ Chapter 07:00 ∞

CODE-BREAKING

As soon as I wake up the next morning, I know one thing for sure. I'm NOT going to school. If I go to school today, I might go into shutdown with everything that happened yesterday. It wasn't the physical challenge of leaping in time or jumping sideways into the trees to avoid being killed by the hitcar, it was EMOTIONAL overload. The shock of MC^2 being put in prison; GMT admitting she used to be a cat burglar; and the hardest part of all, me pretending to be a cat burglar for The Vicious Circle, unable to shout out the truth. Pretending to be someone else, someone not autistic, has exhausted me. When autistic people act like they're not autistic to fit in, they call it masking. I was double-masking yesterday; not being true to myself AND wearing an actual disguise.

I did a brilliant job at keeping quiet. I don't think anyone suspected me. But it cost me. This morning, I can hardly get out of bed. And I know, without trying to speak, that I'm tongue-tied. If I was feeling a bit stronger, I'd THINK about trying to get the Infinity-Glass back. It's Tuesday, the theft only happened yesterday morning, yet we have to find it soon and prove MC^2 is innocent before his trial. They haven't set a date yet; we need to find strong evidence to set him free before they find evidence to convict him. But I must look after myself. I need rest and total quiet.

I used to live under the table on days like this, the tablecloth like the walls of a tent. I'm too tall to do that now so I sit on my sofa bed, and pull the white sheet completely over me. I have my Chronophone and laptop in case I want to contact someone but no one's going to contact me. I know I won't be disturbed by Grandma because she's sleeping in after the extra cleaning job she did last night. I wish she didn't have to do it – her leg is paining her again – but we need the money. The landlord put the rent up but the flat's more run-down than ever.

Big Ben often texts me at breaktime when I'm not in but today he's on a maths trip so won't be texting till lunchtime. And I won't be disturbed by Mrs C Eckler because she's already responded to my text telling her I need time-out today.

My brain's playing tricks on me. It happens when I'm over-stimulated and my brain ought to let me relax but instead it latches onto something and keeps repeating it. Sometimes it's my favourite visual of all time, the black-and-white film of Bob Beamon's record-breaking long jump in Mexico City, 1968; sometimes it's a catchy song lyric and it doesn't matter whether I like it or not, I can't get it out of my head; and sometimes, like now, it's a sentence.

This is what I hear: 'France is 1752' in the voice of MC^2.

Everything about it is wrong. It doesn't make any sense: you can't allocate a year to a country. And why a leap year? And why 1752? But it MUST relate to the theft.

MC^2 wasn't himself when he said it. He was MC^2 minus the Squared! So maybe he was talking gibberish. Or maybe it's a brilliant clue and I have to work it out.

His VOICE was all wrong. It sounded distorted, like he was underwater. It was too quiet; it was too slow. He was running on empty. I repeat the words in my own voice, in my head, to drown out his.

France is 1752. FRANCE is 1752. France IS 1752.

No. Changing the emphasis doesn't help. I put my Chronophone into note mode. Something's niggling me. I need to see the words outside my head. Then, maybe, I can start to make sense of them. I write them down in a circle like this:

and I'm reminded of The Vicious Circle, 12 figures. Maybe MC^2 knows something about The Vicious Circle. He certainly knows a lot about Millennia; he used to work for her at the Time Squad, in the future. I know that sounds impossible but it's normal for Leaplings to work in the past, present or future.

I wish I had Big Ben here to help me. He's very good at problem-solving. Big Ben would latch onto the numbers. He thinks more in numbers than in words. He sees patterns other people don't see. But I don't think this is about maths, it's about logic. Big Ben says logic is a type of maths. What does 1752 MEAN? A unique leap year but what else? Why didn't MC^2 say France is 1616 or 1884 or 2000? I'm stuck on 1752.

I can't think like Big Ben. I can only think like me. I love words, the sight, the sound and the feel of them. MC^2 likes words too but he's more into the SOUND. That's why he's an MC! And yesterday, he didn't sound like himself when he said 'France is . . .' I imagine how he would normally say it. He'd rap it, run his words together, yet every syllable would be crisp.

'France is, France-is, Francis.'

Of course! It was never two words, it was one and the word was FRANCIS. I've cracked half the code. Brilliant! I don't need to go to France, I can solve the mystery here!

Francis 1752. Maybe Francis is the real thief and he lives in 1752. But how would MC^2 know he was the thief? Francis must be one of his friends. And 1752 is still too vague. There must be hundreds of Francises who live in 1752. Which one would it be?

My Chronophone begins to buzz but I ignore it. It isn't a number I recognise. It stops buzzing and a number comes up onto the screen: **1984** and beneath it, Unknown. I wonder who it was. Certainly a Leapling who has a strong connection with 1984.

Chronophones only use four-digit numbers; the Time Squad number was 2000. Four-digit numbers. Of course! It's so obvious I didn't even think of it: 1752 must be a telephone number! Francis 1752 is Francis's telephone number. And he's likely to live in 1752, too!

I check my phone. The person left a message. I don't feel like listening to someone's voice right now. I've spent the past half-hour with voices in my head: MC^2 underwater, my own voice, MC^2 rapping. Now I've cracked the code, there's no time to waste. I create a new contact: FRANCIS, type in 1752 and press save. Then I text:

MC squared is in prison. I'm his friend Elle. Can you help? Concentrating hard on the year 1752, I press send. And then I start shaking. What have I done? Maybe I've just texted the criminal! But it's too late now, I can't intercept it. It must have hit their inbox already. It will have automatically gone to the same date as now in 1752: the 22nd of June.

I walk into the kitchen for a glass of water. When I sit down at the kitchen table, I'm reminded of sitting at the table last night with Big Ben and GMT. I feel bad, sad; the sadness is a physical pain in my chest. I shouted at GMT. She must hate me now. I want to make things better but I'm still not sure whether I can trust her.

But maybe I have no choice. I think of The Infinites ceremony we had in 2048: Kwesi, GMT and MC^2, already Level 3 Infinites; Big Ben and me, Level 1 new recruits; Noon, Eve and Ama as witnesses. Noon and Eve are Leapling twins from 1924 and Ama is Kwesi's Annual sister. I was SO happy. Then I think how different it is today: MC^2 in prison, unable to rap; Kwesi's text, **Don't do nothing without me** but we went behind his back; GMT banished from my flat; and me, off school and alone. Only Big Ben's having a good time. I need my space but I miss my friends. And they're not only friends, they're talented crime-fighters who ROOT FOR THE FUTURE. I can't lie to them or keep back vital information. Finally, I think of The Vicious Circle sitting around the table, arguing amongst themselves. We don't want to end up like that, evil and dishonest and hating each other.

I send a mega-text to all The Infinites:

URGENT MEET THE MUSH-ROOMS AT 4 TODAY

We can't let The Vicious Circle win!

∞

The meeting starts badly!

Kwesi's cross we did the exact opposite of what he told us.

GMT looks only at the damp patch behind the television where mushrooms grow every winter.

Big Ben only wants to talk about the Leaping Lamborghini because he's been overstimulated at his maths day and always talks about cars to decompress.

But when I tell them about Millennia and the ancient-infant called The Grandfather and the mystery number Eight who cast the winning vote, things get much better.

Kwesi high-fives me, GMT smiles and Big Ben repeats, 'You're brave, not scared.'

We plan another meeting for the following night to work out

how to get the Infinity-Glass back. We can't meet earlier because Big Ben and I must attend the Music, Maths and Movement, aka Triple M, Activity Day. There were hundreds of applications for only 24 places. I got on for my outstanding sprinting and Big Ben for his maths talent. We'd be letting our school down if we pulled out. Kwesi now agrees MC^2 was right after all: Big Ben and I should take the lead. I can see by his face he's still uncomfortable about something but impressed what we've achieved so far, considering we're only Level 1s. He signs, ending with ∞ 8.

'You've proved you're fit for Level 2. Next time, bring the Glass back.'

I make everyone leave when I hear Grandma struggling with her keys at the front door. But I feel warm and fuzzy inside. The Infinites are on the right track. But as I open the door to Grandma, who sings, 'Elle Bíbi Imbelé' like she always does when she's in a good mood, I remember something.

In all the craziness, I forgot to tell them about Francis 1752.

I look at my phone again and do big-eyes. I have to sit down at the table. There are two texts. One from Mrs C Eckler apologising for phoning earlier on her husband's Chronophone, asking if I'm OK and reminding me about the Triple M Activity Day tomorrow. The other's from Francis!

Greetings, Elle! Can you visit me in 1752?

So Francis DOES live in 1752 as well as having the year as his phone number. Maybe he knows something about the theft of the Infinity-Glass. I must visit him but I can't do it alone. Leaping back in time is very VERY dangerous. You should really do it with a grown-up but we can't tell grown-ups about The Infinites or our mission because it's top secret. I know one thing: I must tell the others, not by text, but face-to-face tomorrow evening.

We must meet Francis in 1752!

∞ Chapter 08:00 ∞

ANNO, ANON AND NONA

The Music, Maths and Movement School is on the opposite side of town to Intercalary International. It hasn't opened to pupils yet; it's still in development. They invite local pupils as guinea pigs to test their ideas out. This is the first of their Wednesday Summer Activity Days. The main building reminds me of the eco-style buildings from 2048 that we saw last year. It has huge windows to let in the light and the wooden panels on the outside of the building look like bamboo!

We have to get there by bus because it's not a Leapling-only school. We can't just appear out of thin air in front of the building. That would be breaking our Oath of Secrecy because Annuals might see us. But the school is co-founded by Anno, who gave the talk on the Infinity-Glass at the museum, and she's a Leapling. I hope we get a chance to use The Gift today.

Big Ben and I hook up with Jake and Maria at the entrance since we're in the same group. I'm glad they've kept all the Leaplings together so we can be more open about what we say and do. There are 24 visiting pupils divided into six colour-coded groups of four. We're in the silver group taken by Anno. Today she's dressed more like a teacher, in a black trouser suit and white blouse, but her hair's like a sculpture of the Empire State Building!

She addresses all 24 of us.

'Welcome to the Music, Maths and Movement School. I am Anno, one of the co-founders and Director of Movement. There will be no whole-group sessions; we believe in smaller group learning. We will begin with movement. This is how we staff start our days: yoga or dance or running to stimulate the brain. We want our students to have a head start on the day, too. Enjoy your first session.'

Anno leads the four of us outside the main doors, we turn left and follow the building round. I notice she's walking quite close to me and it feels a bit uncomfortable but I don't want to tell her to move further away, it might come out wrong. Then she says something surprising.

'Elle, I was very shocked to witness the theft of the Infinity-Glass on Monday. And I'm very sorry to hear about your friend, MC^2. He visited us here in the future, helped us develop the core curriculum for Movement. I believe he is innocent. If there's anything we can do to help, don't hesitate to ask.'

I'm surprised she knows we're friends. She certainly doesn't know we're INFINITES. But the Leapling community is tiny and word travels fast.

'Thank you,' I say, hoping she will give me some space now but she doesn't.

'I know Kwesi and Ama, too, of course. I keep track of exceptional pupils across the timeline. Ama is lined up for a career in robot design and Kwesi's created outstanding murals since leaving our school. They excel at athletics, too.'

'Kwesi calls himself Visual ASD. For him, ASD stands for Autistic Street Designer. He speaks his own sign language. And he's so fluent in Standard Sign Language, he does presentations at international art exhibitions in the future.'

'Indeed, he is very creative. I paint myself but sculpture's my thing. You'll see some later.' She stops walking for a second and checks her watch. 'We have tried to create an inclusive school that nurtures autistic people's skills and minimises sensitivities as well as catering for pupils with different or minimal challenges. We are meeting our goals in the mid-21st century. Kwesi benefitted.'

'Do you travel to the future often?'

'All the time. It's cheating but why not use The Gift to develop the best educational programme? We're light years ahead of contemporary schools. But some of the ideas are stuff we already know in the present.'

'What do you mean?'

'We know sitting at desks doesn't always get the best results; that many students benefit from rhythmic learning; and maths makes more sense in the real world. But it's hard to break old traditions.'

We turn a corner and I forget she's still in my personal space. My eyes go bigger than Jupiter, Big Ben starts stimming with excitement, Maria swears in Portuguese in a good way and Jake whoops. I thought the athletics track at Intercalary International was good but this is like an Olympic stadium! The track is orange, obviously brand new and has covered, raked seats all the way round.

'I've never seen an orange track before,' I say, thinking aloud.

'It's an eco-friendly surface and international standard. It'll give you extra spring,' says Anno, smiling. 'We'll be paying it off for decades but it's worth every penny. Take a run on it.'

'I didn't bring my trainers.'

That's not the only thing that's bothering me. The track looks too perfect to walk on. I don't want to be the first to spoil it. It's like Anno can read my mind.

'Don't worry, it's indestructible. You'll get a good idea, even in shoes.'

Jake's on the track before she's finished her sentence. Maria goes next, followed by Big Ben and me. We're jogging slowly but our stride length is incredible. It's almost TOO bouncy. I wonder how fast I can run the 100 metres here. That must be how the sprinters felt in 1968, the first Olympics on a synthetic track. The perfect surface and high altitude meant they smashed all the records under 800 metres!

When we've done a lap, Anno makes an announcement.

'We're having a closed meet this evening,' she says. 'We have to raise money every way we can to pay for the facilities. But you are all very welcome to participate free, as guest runners. That way we don't need to list your school name.'

The existence of Intercalary International is a secret outside the Leapling community so we don't usually get the opportunity to do interschool sports events. Jake shrugs but Maria says yes immediately. She's a champion high jumper. I look at Big Ben and wonder if he's thinking what I'm thinking. We should really be having a meeting this evening to work out what to do next. I LOVE athletics, it's my specialist subject, but Big Ben and I are on a mission. We mustn't get side-tracked and run out of time.

'I'm busy,' I say. I know that must sound rude but I hate having to choose and feel a bit panicked. My words came out wrong. But Anno isn't offended at all.

'It's totally your choice, Elle. Ama's doing the long jump. And the 100 metres.'

'AMA!'

Kwesi's Annual sister. The friend I haven't seen since last year's school trip to 2048! Ama, now in Tenth Year in 2049. How will they luggage her here?

'She heard you were coming here this week in 2021 and was desperate to see you. We offered to transport her.'

'Who's we?'

'Myself and my co-founder sisters, Anon, Director of Music, and Nona, Director of Maths. You'll meet them in due course.'

Anno, Anon and Nona. I LOVE their anagram names, like the same person with different emphasis. If they had a pet dog, they could call it Nano! Big Ben would like that.

'Are you triplets?'

'Good gracious, no! Anon and I look alike – some people get us confused – but she's 12 years older than me. Nona's the baby.'

'Are you all Leaplings?'

'Anon and I, yes. Nona missed out. But she has her own gift: architecture. She designed this school building.'

Big Ben smiles. 'The odds on two members of the same family being Leaplings is one in two million.'

'I believe so, Ben. Do you know the odds for two Leaplings with The Gift? Anon used to be a talented gymnast but fell off a beam, which affected her mobility. She walks with a stick now.' Anno turns to me. 'Nona's like Ama; swore the Oath but can only leap as luggage. I'm sure Ama will understand how busy you are, Elle.'

My stomach ties up in a knot. It's so difficult to change my mind once I've made a decision. But now I know Ama's coming here, everything's changed. It would be wonderful to see Ama again; we've missed each other loads. And she'll want to race me as much as I want to race her. It would be great fun. AND seeing her do the long jump. That's her best event. Surely there'll still be time to solve the crime, too?

'I'd like to come,' I say.

Anno smiles. 'I thought that might persuade you. What about you, Ben?'

Big Ben nods and I'm pleased. It will be even more fun with Big Ben around.

'Excellent. We have all sizes of the most comfortable kit ever because it's made of a material . . .'

'That hasn't been invented yet!' I smile. I'm already looking forward to this evening.

∞

Assistants give us headphones for the music session before lunch. It's taking place in one of their teaching rooms, a bright, light space with large windows overlooking the athletics stadium. Usually bright lights give me a headache but these ones don't so they must be from the future. The four of us have the option of sitting on seats, standing or walking around. I prefer to sit but Jake and Maria stand and Big Ben does running up and down, stimming to relax. It's nice they let us do what makes us most comfortable. Anno was right; not everyone learns best when they're sitting in a chair. The headphones are amazing. They filter out all the whispering and fidgeting before the session begins. I wish we had them at Intercalary International.

A minute later, a tall woman with black hair streaked with grey and pulled into a tight bun, round bronze glasses and a matching bronze walking stick enters the room. She's wearing a mustard-coloured shiny dress with a tight-fitting bodice and long full-length skirt and cream shoes with buckles on. Maybe she's from the olden days! When she clips the microphone onto her lacy shawl, it spoils the effect.

'Dear Intercalary Intellectuals, I am Anon, as in Anonymous. But anonymous means no name, and Anon IS my name. I am therefore a walking, talking contradiction.'

I smile. Anon likes words as much as I do. And I remember she's a Leapling, so we have that in common as well. She continues.

'I am a famous and unacknowledged poet. Raise your hands if you have heard of me.'

I put my hand up. Anon peers at me through her glasses.

'I believe you are Elle, winner of the 1752 Poetry Prize? What do you know of Anon?'

'I read a poem in an anthology called *Poor Old Lady*, about a woman who swallowed a fly. It was by Anon. But I've heard people sing it with different words.'

Anon slowly nods. 'In the olden days, when poets WROTE poems, they signed their names underneath so people knew they were the author, for example, William Wordsworth. But lots of illiterate people – those who could neither read nor write – made up poems, too. These poems were ORAL, spoken or sung. People learnt them, altered the words across the centuries and editors published different versions in poetry anthologies. Since they knew not who first invented the poems, they attributed them to Anonymous, shortened to Anon.'

'There were lots of poems by Anon in that anthology,' I say. 'But as YOU are Anon, they can't all have been made up by illiterate people. Were some of them written and signed by you and published at different times in history?'

'Indeed they were. But take heed: Annuals know not of my existence. Let this be our secret. What is poetry but a songbird perched on a page? As Director of Music, I fervently believe music and poetry spring from the same muse.'

'If they're all published as Anon, how do we know which ones were written by you?'

'Mine, fellow poet, are the BEST.'

This makes me smile. It was a good joke and I like that she called me a poet and I like her. She's different to anyone I've ever met. I wonder if she's autistic and poetry's her specialist subject.

'I have a passion for poems; they allow words to break the rules. Some believe poetry is putting language in a cage but I believe the opposite. The cage is a liberation. The caged word truly sings!'

'Try telling that to a zoo animal,' says Jake.

'Young man,' Anon fixes him with her round glasses, 'I speak of words not birds. I wish you to listen to an 18th-century poem on your audio-apparatus. Poetry is not merely—'

A mid-teen with bronze skin and short spiky blue-and-green peacock hair pokes her head round the door. Anon blinks behind her glasses, obviously cross.

'What is it, Portia?' She pronounces it Porsha and Big Ben stops running.

'There's a problem.'

'You may speak freely, we are all of us Leaplings.'

'It's 2033. They delivered the wrong robots.'

'The fiddlefaddle future I despise most of all; they make much ado about nothing. Give me the past any day.'

'Intercalaries, this is Portia, my adopted niece. She is named for the heroine in Shakespeare's *The Merchant of Venice* and knows more than she should about music of the past, present and future. She will conduct the remainder of your session.'

∞

Lunch is amazing. They asked us in advance what we'd like so they could arrange a buffet for everyone. They even asked which cakes we liked for later and I gave them the recipe for my favourite vegan coconut cake. We can stick to our preferences or try new things. We're allowed to go up to the counter several times so we don't need to load our plates up with several different kinds of foods at a time like at Intercalary International. That's one of the reasons I always take sandwiches. I like to know exactly what I'm going to have to eat and make sure it's the right kind. When I eat mozzarella in white flatbread it has to be a particular brand of mozzarella and a particular brand of flatbread. If not, it tastes wrong, sometimes so wrong I can't eat it.

Portia's sitting with the Intercalary International pupils in case we want to ask any secret questions about time-travel because she's a Leapling, too. She's accompanied her mum, Anno, and aunt, Anon, on numerous trips on the timeline. When I go up to the counter the second time, I notice her tall, slim figure next to me. She sees me looking at the beetroot.

'It's the best colour EVER,' I say, 'but I'd have to close my eyes to eat it. Maybe it's just a feast for the eyes.' That's what Mrs C Eckler calls all the foods I like the look of but find too bright to eat.

'No need,' says Portia, 'if you wear these.'

She produces some pink plastic sunglasses from her bag. They look like something from a toy shop but who knows. I put them on and instantly the beetroot looks grey. They've made everything go black and white.

'Now it looks horrible,' I say and she laughs.

'They're colour-coolers. If you press the left button,' she shows me the inside of the hinge, 'it changes the shade. The right button changes the colour. You can make it white if you want.'

It works! I carry the plate back to my seat. The beetroot tastes very intense, the vinegar is sweet and kind of explodes in my mouth like sherbet and I like it a lot. But I would never have been able to eat it if it looked purple. Maybe one day I will.

'Can I keep these?'

'Of course.'

Big Ben eats three plates of food! Then he bombards Portia with questions.

'Have you been to 2033? What is it like? Why are the robots wrong?'

I've never seen Big Ben so animated and I feel a tight feeling in my stomach. I'm scared Big Ben likes Portia more than me; I want him to like me best. I'm jealous. Portia's too old for him. She looks the same age as GMT, 4-leap +1. But she answers all Big Ben's questions without rolling her eyes clockwise or anti-clockwise like some people do so she's not a bad person. I just find it difficult to like her as much as I thought because of the effect she's having on Big Ben.

When lunch is over, Portia shows the four of us several of their relaxation rooms for pupils who need 1-2-1 lessons or have Special Educational Needs. There's a SENsory Room like there was at the Time Squad Centre in 2048 with a couple of white tents inside, lots of cushions and sequinned drapes I have to squint my eyes sideways to totally appreciate; the Lyrical Lounge, which has poems and song lyrics written all over the walls that I find the opposite of relaxing but Portia loves; and the Clashroom, which looks more like a traditional classroom with wooden tables and chairs.

The first session after lunch will be maths. They announce an Oops: the sessions will now be in two groups of 12 rather than six groups of four because some of the group leaders had to leave. In spite of that, Big Ben's really excited because it's his specialist subject. We're in group one. We line up outside the classroom, all the Intercalaries plus eight pupils from other schools. We hear a door close at the end of the corridor and a woman wearing a black trouser suit begins walking towards us. She swings her arms like she's marching, but her shoes don't make any sound at all on the futuristic surface. She has short black hair, and looks like she's about to launch a shot put at us. I gasp and my eyes go bigger than Jupiter as the realisation hits me.

This must be Nona – none other than Evil Nine!

∞ Chapter 09:00 ∞

MELTDOWN

I t's a large square room with a clock on the wall and a teacher's desk underneath where Nona sits. In the middle of the room, 12 chairs are arranged in a circle.

'Sit!' says Nona, like we're dogs.

We all sit down. I make sure Big Ben and I sit furthest away from Nona. I don't want to be anywhere near her and I certainly don't want her speaking to my back. It must be weird for the pupils on the other side of the circle. If this was The Vicious Circle, we'd be 6 and 7. I try to banish the thought from my mind. I want to tell Big Ben who she is but don't want to get into trouble for talking. Actually, I want to leave and hide in the SENsory Room but it wouldn't be fair to abandon Big Ben. Although maths is his favourite subject, he doesn't like meeting new people and so much has been new for us today.

Nona stands up behind her chair. 'I am Nona, architect and Director of Mathematics. Tell me your names, starting with you.'

She's looking straight at me and I feel the blood rushing to my face. It feels like a physical pain. I take a deep breath and look at the floor.

'Elle,' I say.

'Welcome, Elle. I thought you might enjoy the familiar set-up, 12 chairs in a circle.'

Oh my Chrono! She knows it was ME in disguise at The Vicious Circle. I feel physically sick yet super strong at the same time. What will she do to me? I delivered the Infinity-Glass to them; I failed in my mission to get it back to the museum. I've done The Vicious Circle a favour. Surely she can't exit me in front of the other students however evil she is?

Once all 12 of us have said our names, Nona continues. 'Raise your hands if you know what Nona means.'

Some of the pupils raise their hands. I know the answer but if I said it, I might collapse to the ground with its sinister meaning.

'Noon?' says Jake.

It's not a bad guess; Noon was on the Time Squad Centre trip last year. But Jake didn't put his hand up, as usual.

'No hand, invalid answer. Even if it's correct.'

Nona picks one of the girls.

'Noon?' she says.

'Incorrect,' says Nona. 'Nona means nine or the ninth. From the Latin.'

I take very slow deep breaths to remain calm. Big Ben raises his hand.

'Did your parents call you Nine? Or you chose it?'

'My parents did not call me Nine. They called me Nona. Nine is the best number but not the best name.'

'Why is 9 your best number?'

'It's the square of 3 and the rotation of 6. If you keep adding the digits in the 9 times table until they are reduced to a single digit, that digit is always 9. But enough of my opinion. I want to hear from all of you. Choose a favourite number between 1 and 9.' She pauses for ten seconds. 'Elle, we'll begin with you.'

She's definitely trying to intimidate me by making me go first twice. But it has the opposite effect. Although it takes me by surprise, which is hard, it means I can get it over and done with. No time to get anxious about when she's going to pick me.

'8,' I say, then to show her I mean business, I take a deep breath and give her my best Elle stare, 'because it's symmetrical and beautiful and looks like an hourglass!'

Nona is lost for words. Now I've taken her by surprise. Elle, 1: Nona, nil! Of course, no one, not even Big Ben, has any idea what's going on. I haven't had the chance to tell him she's Evil Nine. Nona clears her throat to try to get her voice back and buy time. Then she continues.

'Ben, your favourite number? Between 1 and 9.'

Big Ben's shaking his head. 'My favourite number is 0.6 recurring.'

Only 0.6 recurring of Leaplings have The Gift. That's why it's Big Ben's favourite number. He knows not to say this in front of Annuals, though. His favourite number is so important to him that he can't concentrate on anything else.

'Ben, that is incorrect. I SAID between 1 and 9. 0.6 recurring is less than 1. I might add, it must be a whole number. Not a fraction or a decimal. 1, 2, 3, 4, 5, 6, 7, 8, or 9. Take your pick!'

'What about 0?'

'What about it?'

'It's a number.'

'It's not between 1 and 9. Pick a favourite number between—'

'My favourite number is 0.6 recurring!'

'Do NOT interrupt.'

'What about 0?'

'We're going round in circles.'

Big Ben is rocking in his chair. 'My favourite number is 0.666666—'

'SILENCE!'

Big Ben stops rocking and stands up abruptly. I know the sign and stand up too. He's not repeating himself to be naughty; he's upset and confused and he's saying his favourite number to calm down. He's on the verge of a meltdown. I look at Nona and am shocked to see she's smiling. She shouted deliberately to upset Big Ben. Evil Nine is living up to her name!

'Count,' I tell him, keeping my voice calm and steady though I don't feel calm at all. Big Ben's gone rigid. He's trying to hold it in but the normal strategies, deep breaths, counting, aren't going to work for long. Not here, in front of total strangers.

I raise my hand. 'Please can we have time-out? He needs—'

'He needs to do as he's told.'

'That's not fair. He's autistic and he loves maths and you humiliated him!'

As I'm speaking, I hear a couple of pupils from the other schools gasp aloud, Maria swearing under her breath, Big Ben counting, and at the same time, feel Nona's cat's eyes burning into me. Before she can say anything else, I say to Big Ben, 'Time-out in the Clashroom,' and lead him out of the room. I block out Nona's shouting and focus only on the task.

When we reach the Clashroom, Big Ben is shaking, beyond words, beyond numbers. He picks up one of the chairs and throws it at the whiteboard. Of course, it doesn't break. It's been designed to withstand knocks, like the ones in Big Ben's Anger Management workshops. Big Ben's not an angry person at all but he goes from 0 to 10 on the anger scale when people are insensitive to him. In this case, Nona was deliberately cruel! Big Ben goes from sadness and humiliation to frustration to anger. Being autistic means he can't cope with the emotional overload and he has a physical response. He's getting better at doing time-out when he's overloaded but this was totally unexpected and happened too quickly for him to notice he was growing tense.

After a while, he calms down and curls up in the corner, making soft, moaning noises, which is his way of soothing himself. Thank goodness we managed to get out of the session. I see a face at the door. Portia. She opens it very slowly and motions me over.

'How is he?'

'He had a meltdown.'

'I know.'

'How? You weren't in the room.' I wish my voice sounded more normal but speaking to Portia makes me nervous. It's because Big Ben likes her so much.

'We watched it back on the video. Cameras in all the rooms here. Like CCTV.'

It's then that I notice them in this room too. I remember Ama telling me about them in 2048. They don't have any bullying at the Triple M School because all the evidence is on camera. Cameras can't stop 100% of it though. Bullies like Nona don't care if they're filmed or not.

'Nona humiliated him and shouted at him in front of people he doesn't know.'

'Are you happy to stay here with him? Anything you need?'

'Just some water. Please.'

'Water coming up. I'll come and get you both at teatime. That should give Big Ben enough quiet time. The cakes are looking good; don't want him to miss out!'

∞

Portia returns just after 4.

'Anon and Anno wish to speak to you both in their office. Follow me.'

Is it my imagination or does Portia sound less friendly, more like a teacher? She called Anno by name rather than mum. I'm worried now. Maybe Big Ben and I will get into trouble for doing time-out without permission, even though Nona was in the wrong.

Big Ben and I follow Portia along the corridor and up some stairs. The office is at the end of another corridor. It's a room within a room with a waiting area outside where Portia tells us to sit down; then she leaves. I look up into the corner of the room. No cameras! And probably no cameras inside the office either. Anno, Anon and Nona don't want their private meetings recorded.

I can hear their voices coming from the office. They're talking about the maths session. I try not to listen but it's difficult not to; my hearing's so good, I often hear what people are saying in the next room. I remind myself I'm a Level 1 Infinite on a job. I need to catch up with Big Ben. I don't know how much time we'll have to talk 1-2-1 and this is the only place in the building where our speech won't be recorded.

'BB. Nona's Evil Nine!'

'She said her favourite number was 9.'

'It is. But I mean she's Nine in The Vicious Circle!'

He does big-eyes. 'Is it evidence?'

'Maybe. But there's something else.'

I tell him how I worked out France is was Francis and show him the message:

Greetings, Elle! Can you visit me in 1752?

I can see he's impressed.

'Did you text back?'

'No. I wanted to show you first. We need to work together. I think we should leap to 1752.'

'We need a date and time and place.'

'Logical,' I say and Big Ben smiles, hearing his favourite word.

'I'll text him to—'

At that moment the voices in the room become raised and even Big Ben's able to hear.

'Do NOT use that word!' It's Anon, as in Anonymous. 'Why do you persist in tormenting me?'

'ECCENTRIC,' says Nona. 'Say what you will, that's what you are.'

'That word is anathema to me. I shudder to hear it. I am offended by its inaccuracy! I am NOT off centre, I am completely OUTSIDE the circle. I am AUTISTIC and proud of it, as the young lady and gentleman should be.'

'Always for the underdog,' says Nona.

'Indeed I am. This is an INCLUSIVE school, Nona. And in this space, you abide by Music, Maths and Movement rules. You will apologise to Elle and Big Ben—'

'I'll do nothing of the—'

'—or tender your resignation!'

There's a long silence, some murmuring even I can't hear, then the door suddenly opens and it's Anno who smiles at us, her Empire State Building hair-do showing the odd stray hair but still impressive.

'Elle. Big Ben. I didn't realise you were outside already. Please come inside.'

As we walk in, I hear Nona murmur, 'Eavesdropping!' She really is the vilest woman I've ever met, apart from Millennia. Anon stands using her walking stick as we enter. She gives us a wide smile.

'On behalf of the Music, Maths and Movement School, we apologise profusely for the unfortunate incident in your mathematics session. My fellow co-founder, Nona, wishes to address you individually.'

There's another pause. 'Ben, I am sorry I shouted at you. I should have respected your favourite number. Elle, I am sorry for not allowing you time-out and shouting at you, too.'

If we hadn't just overheard their argument, I'd believe Nona really is sorry. But I know she's only saying it to keep her job. It was nice hearing Anon stick up for us, though. As I guessed, she's autistic like us and would understand why we behaved as we did. How can such a nice person be related to someone like Nona? Anno speaks now.

'I do hope you've had time to get your strength back and will join us for tea in the canteen?'

Before we can answer, Anon intervenes.

'Oh, no. The canteen will be a tempest of teacups. I have another establishment in mind, same date, superior year. Follow me!'

'A tempest of teacups, indeed?' says Anno, in Anon's voice. 'Well, Intercalaries, you are very welcome to see my sculptures in the Art Department after tea. And, if you have the energy, still take part in the athletics meet.'

'Yes, please, Anno. We're both very keen,' I say. I still can't wait to see Ama again and compete against her. It will be a nice way to end the day after the clash with Evil Nine.

'Come along now, dears,' says Anon and ushers us out of the room with her walking stick, past the chairs and along the corridor, downstairs back to the Clashroom. I hope we're not going to have tea in here but a different time frame! Big Ben is more optimistic.

'Where are we going? Is there cakes?'

'At the place we are visiting, the tea is quite excellent,' says Anno, 'but there will be no cake provided. The Master takes breakfast at noon, declares lunch is "as much food as one's hand can hold", and dines late. Therefore, I have packed a generous hamper from the canteen so we are all set for leaping.'

'Leaping!' I say. 'Anon, please tell us where we're going. I HATE surprises.'

'Sorry, my fellow time-travellers, I have been remiss.' Anon stops walking and adjusts her glasses. 'We are going to Gough Square, close to London's famous Fleet Street where the first daily newspapers were published. I have engineered an invitation for us all to take tea on this very date at my dear friend Samuel's residence in 1752. Now I'm approaching half a century, I find same date leaps easier to accomplish. Samuel is the leader of the London literati: highly educated specialists in literature. And he is a poet. As a prizewinning poet, Elle, you will appreciate this greatly and Big Ben will enjoy his company.' She pauses. 'He is a generous host. You have both had an unfortunate experience; I hope this restores your faith in adults!'

I look at Big Ben; Big Ben looks at me. I know he's thinking what I'm thinking. 1752. Absolutely perfect for our mission.

∞ Chapter 10:00 ∞

THE LITERATI

Anon should have warned us about the stench! I've always been sensitive to smell but this is an out-of-order toilet to the power of 3! But it's 1752; I have to rise to the challenge. I breathe through my mouth and Anon offers us leap sweets to help with the travel sickness, which I gladly accept. Apple! She accidentally drops her wrapper on the ground.

'That should fortify you, Elle,' she says, 'but please recover that errant litter. I am too stiff, alas, to retrieve it. These pavements are filthy but their dirt, unlike ours, is biodegradable.'

I pick up the wrapper and slowly take in my surroundings. The three of us are standing in an alley which Anon confirms is just off Fleet Street, close to the house we're visiting. On the Fleet Street side, there are people shouting and the sound of horses, but the other end is quiet. I hope we're taking the peaceful route! We had to leap to this spot to not draw too much attention to ourselves. But we didn't escape people completely. Sitting on the ground is a person dressed in grey rags, a very old woman with wrinkles and hair like wisps of white sheep's wool caught on barbed wire. She's clinging to Anon's skirt. Anon places some coins in her free hand and we slowly begin to walk.

'That's Old Meg,' she says. 'She has seen better days and more Chronos than you or I can imagine! She calls Leaplings ghosts, apparitions. We can trust she will not disclose our secret since she makes more money from us in a week than the entire population of Annuals in a year. But 'tis a hard life. I am surprised dear Samuel has not offered her a lodging.'

'Is your friend a landlord?'

'No, Elle. His name is Mr Johnson but you can also address him as Sir. He will, in time, be honoured with the title Dr Johnson, revered as a literary legend, but it hasn't happened to him yet. He's the kindest man I have encountered on the time-line, perceiving goodness where others see guilt. His house is brimming with unfortunates.'

I know it sounds unkind but I'm not sure I'm going to enjoy having tea at Mr Johnson's house if there are lots of other people there. It will be overwhelming, especially if they want to make conversation. We pass a well-dressed couple in the street and they stare intently at me, not at Anon or Big Ben. It suddenly hits me that they're staring because I'm black. This makes me uncomfortable. I was so excited about visiting 1752, I didn't think about how people might view me differently. I wonder how many black people live in London in 1752 compared to 2021?

I'm also not enjoying walking along the street in the clothes Anon lent me. I'm wearing an outfit similar to hers but in pale yellow with a full-length skirt and brown buckled shoes. Thankfully, nothing's itchy but I don't feel like myself because I usually wear trousers or athletics kit. It's like I'm in disguise again. Big Ben looks really odd in his outfit because breeches are supposed to be like long shorts but his are above the knee. Anon couldn't find any that fit properly.

Soon, we reach a smart-looking square of tall terraced houses with long windows. They look old-fashioned and modern at the same time – modern here in 1752 but reminding me of old-fashioned houses in 2021. When we reach the closest house on the left-hand corner, Anon climbs the grand steps and knocks on the door. Big Ben and I wait at the bottom. I can hear his stomach rumbling. I hope Anon brought some nice cakes in the hamper. The door opens abruptly and a woman about the same age as Anon but shorter, wearing a white cloth cap, peers out. She seems to be squinting at us more than Anon.

'Who are you?'

'You know very well who I am. I am Anon, as in Anonymous, the poet, accompanied by my young adventurers, Mistress Elle and Master Ben. We have come to see—'

'Go away!' says the woman and slams the door.

Big Ben and I look at each other. My heart is almost leaping out of my chest. The woman doesn't like us. We need to leap back NOW. But Anon has other ideas. She walks back down the steps with the help of her stick.

'That was Mistress Anna Williams, the housekeeper. An ill-tempered, well-read gentlewoman who occasionally excels in poetry. Alas, her sight is failing and Mr Johnson employed her as housekeeper here because he values her company and intellect. She can see enough to perform her duties and is able to read with the aid of spectacles. She deems herself his favourite. She is mistaken, as you will discover.'

Anon looks up to the first-floor left-hand window and we follow her gaze. There's a tall, broad man wearing a white wig like judges wear. His head is tilted to one side like he's about to do the shot put and he's shaking it continuously. I think he's also telling us not to come in but suddenly he waves his hand and Anon waves back. Then she walks back up the steps and waits. A minute later, Mistress Anna opens the door again, slowly this time and looks away from us.

'The Master will see you.'

We're shown to a dingy, brown-painted, panelled room on the right-hand side and told to wait for instructions. Big Ben's too restless to sit down.

'When will we have cake?'

'Very soon, my dear,' says Anon. 'Dear Samuel is exceedingly fond of drinking tea and although it is not yet the fashion to accompany afternoon tea with cake, he has an appetite for it to match your own. We will be called upstairs once tea is served. I can hear the cacophony of crockery in the kitchen below. This house has few rules but they take tea very seriously.'

'What are the other rules?' I say.

'When you meet Mr Johnson, you must curtsy to him. And you, Big Ben, must bow. That is the norm for the 18th century. In all other respects, Mr Johnson is casual for a man of his time.'

The sound of clomping footsteps up and down the stairs is

strangely reassuring. Mistress Anna is still cross but at least she's carrying the tea set from the basement kitchen. She must find everything extra tricky if she's blind like I find things challenging because I'm autistic. Ten minutes later, we follow her up the winding staircase and enter a room on the right with pale green walls, much brighter and nicer than the waiting room. She announces us and opens a cupboard on the far side of the room.

The large man in the white wig is staring out from the same window as before, shaking his head and waving. Even from this distance, I can smell his sweat. His wig is a dirty grey colour, singed at the edges, and his shirt's stained with what looks like faded black ink. He's waving like Anon's still there. I wonder for a moment if Anon has leapt twice, once now and the other on a different occasion and is playing tricks on him. But then I realise he's not MEANING to wave at all. His hand can't stop waving. He's tapping his feet, too, muttering to himself under his breath, then suddenly he blows out a loud whistle. I'm mesmerised and a bit scared of him at the same time.

Abruptly, he turns, like a shot putter in the circle and speaks in a loud, booming voice that makes me jump:

'Anon, what is it of the clock?'

'Four in the afternoon, Sir,' says Anon, with a curtsy.

'Then it is time for tea. Before I made your acquaintance, I took tea morning, noon and night. Now I have taken to indulging in the afternoon; I am a hardened and shameless tea drinker. Pray, be seated, one and all. What is your name, boy?'

'Big Ben,' says Big Ben with a bow, without pausing at all.

I'm surprised he answered straight away and used his nick-name, rather than his christened name, Benedykt. He must like Mr Johnson already. That's a good sign; Big Ben's very good at judging character.

'A befitting name for a fine fellow!'

I'm glad Mr Johnson likes Big Ben, too. I curtsy to him like Anon told me. I've been concentrating on Mr Johnson so intensely, especially his eyes. One of them seems half closed and the other is squinting. Now I see what Anon meant about them taking tea seriously. They don't serve it in mugs. On the table in front of us Mistress Anna has placed an elaborate china tea set, white with pink flowers; the teacups are tiny, with no handles at all. Mistress Anna takes an oak box out of the cupboard which looks a bit chipped and almost drops it beside the tea set. It has a lock on it. I wonder what's inside? Maybe it's jewels. It must be something very precious. Then she unlocks it with a tiny silver key and the smell overpowers me. Tea! I should have guessed.

Once Mistress Anna has added the tea leaves and hot water to the teapot, locked the box and put it back in the cupboard, Mr Johnson pours cups for everyone. He offers us milk and sugar and drinks down his own immediately. I politely refuse both, take a sip of the liquid and almost spit it out – it's so bitter! And the cup burns my hand! Maybe milk helps to make it taste better AND cool it down. Then I notice Anon has poured hers into the saucer to allow it to cool quicker so I do the same. There are two large plates and a pile of small matching ones. Big Ben looks at Anon and she reads his mind.

'Oh, I almost forgot the hamper.' She lays out a selection of cakes onto the large plates and a knife. 'Elle, I have brought your favourite coconut cake. Sir, would you care for a slice?' Anon busies herself with serving.

I take a bite of the coconut cake: delicious! I try not to focus too closely on my host but I can't help myself. Although the tea set is posh, Mr Johnson's eating is not! He stuffs food into his mouth and the crumbs fall more on his clothes than the plate. He constantly refills his teacup and twice stretches out his arm whilst still holding the tea, spilling most of it on the floor! Even though his manner is gruff and his voice loud, I begin to feel relaxed. He is being himself, not pretending to be polite; we can be ourselves too. He seems to particularly like the coconut sponge.

'An extraordinary mind makes extraordinary cake. Did you cook this?'

He's addressing me! My face instantly burns red with the unexpectedness.

'No, Sir.'

'What is your name?'

'Elle.'

'The French for she, a palindrome, what better?
The letter L becomes my favourite letter.'

I'm pleased he noticed my name is a palindrome, love that he made it into a rhyme but not sure if I'm supposed to reply. I say nothing; he peers closely at me.

94

'You do not know what to make of me, Elle. I am in perpetual motion. My intellect mirrors my body; thoughts animate me. Furthermore, Anon informs me my voice is harsh. I may bark but I don't bite.'

Although his face is twitching, he gives me a twinkling smile. I like Mr Johnson. He can't help his body spasms any more than I can help it when I repeat phrases out loud or Big Ben stims by running up and down. I don't think he's autistic though. I'll ask Anon later. She takes a sip of her tea.

'How goes the Dictionary, Sir? On my previous visit, you had barely reached Bamboo!'

'Ah, the Dictionary. I was for a long time BAMBOOZLED but now I am merely PERPLEXED by the length of the under-taking.'

'You have reached the letter P?'

'I have indeed. And illuminated some meanings with several extracts from your poems I recall from memory.'

'You are too kind.'

'*Verba volant, scripta manent*: spoken words fly away but written remain.'

'Sir, I glow with pleasure when you quote Latin. Please permit Elle and Big Ben a glance at your great work?'

'Why, of course.' He stands up. 'If you follow the stairs up until you can rise no further, you will find yourselves in the garret. There, my scribes will keep you occupied . . .'

∞

The garret is a word paradise!

It's a huge, long, light room the length of the whole house, with piles and piles of brown hardback books scattered all over the place and covered in dust. Some of the piles are so high they're like sculptures! I've never seen so many books outside a library! They're old and faded with battered spines. Mr Johnson's books are like his clothes. Several men are standing at a long table copying out passages from books in beautiful, sloping, old-fashioned handwriting onto slips of paper. Everything's larger than life; I feel tiny, even though I'm tall for my age. Halfway along the wall is a writing desk with an inkpot on it and a very large chair with only three legs which must be where Mr Johnson sits.

One of the men comes over, a short stocky man in a clean white wig who looks much younger than Mr Johnson.

'You must be friends of young Frank,' he says and before we can correct him or ask who young Frank is, 'come in, come in and see words at work!'

On the table are sheets of paper nearly two feet high with slips of paper all over them, covered with written extracts from poems.

'I thought it was a dictionary, not a poetry anthology.'

I know that sounds rude but I wasn't expecting that at all. Mr Johnson just said he'd used extracts from Anon's poems but all the dictionaries I've seen give definitions of the words in prose.

'Mr Johnson is an expert on poems,' the man explains. 'He is a poet himself and his head is bursting with them. "Why use prose when you can use poetry," he always says. But in my humble opinion, he prefers poems because he can remember them. He has an UNCOMMON memory and is constantly speaking them aloud. We have difficulty keeping apace with him.'

'Why are the pages so big?'

'To fit all the words on, young madam. There will be two volumes, for the first only takes us to the letter K.'

I smile. People accuse me of speaking like I swallowed a dictionary. Imagine if I swallowed this one!

Heavy footsteps are coming up the stairs. Mr Johnson joins us a minute later. He must be fit because he's not out of breath at all. I wonder how fast he can run the 100 metres? I don't ask him though. That would be inappropriate.

'I trust you have occupied my scribes,' he says, 'for I always outtalk and outquote them.'

Big Ben's looking at the pages intently and I'm reminded of his dyslexia. When he tries to read printed books, he says the letters move around like ants crawling across the page. But this handwriting looks so beautiful in blue-black ink, it doesn't matter that you can't read it. Each s looks like an f and there are lots of swirly doodles. I find it hard to read handwriting at the best of times and I LOVE reading. It must be impossible for Big Ben. Handwriting is very different to print.

'Do you tell them what to write down, Mr Johnson?' he says.

'Indeed I do. But they have to check quotations from the library,' he gestures to the piles of books on the floor. 'I pride myself on accuracy but it is the job of the scribes to locate the sources. Shakespeare is simple, but Anonymous a superior chal-lenge.' He smiles.

'What if you made a spelling mistake?'

'They begin over again. But spelling has been a fickle phenomenon, young man. Before dictionaries, you could spell a word every which way you liked. The great playwright himself spelt his name in all manner of abbreviations, and spellings from Shakspere to Shakspeare with an 'a'. And it was printed in many more ways than there are days of the week.

'Nowadays, however, there is a fashion for fixing the language. But take heed, young man: the language refuses to be fixed.'

Big Ben nods. I can tell he likes the idea of spelling things lots of different ways. Maybe now he'll be more open to travelling further back into the past, when people thought differently. Before dictionaries, he'd be less stressed about spelling words wrong.

'Do you have a favourite word in your dictionary, Sir?' I say.

'No, I do not. But here is one for you: backfriend. It means a friend backwards, an enemy in secret. I thought it might appeal since Anon informs me you are a poet inspired by reversing the natural order of things. Beware the backfriend, Elle, but treasure the genuine article. Big Ben is clearly the latter, a true friend.'

'Thank you, Sir,' we say, at exactly the same time.

∞

Later, downstairs, Mr Johnson is unusually quiet. His face and hands are still twitching but he looks like he's aged. He notices me looking at him.

'*Cave canem*, Elle. Beware of the dog. But especially, beware of the black dog, melancholia. Since the death of my dear wife, Tetty, the black dog has been the shadow at my side. Were it not for female company such as Anon and Mistress Anna, I would despair completely.'

'Oh, Mr Johnson, you shouldn't say such things.' Anon adjusts her glasses and I can see she's gone quite pink. 'Surely Frank is a comfort to you?'

Mr Johnson seems to come to life again. 'Ah yes, dearest Frank. Until his arrival, this was my *annus terribilis*, the worst year of my existence. But he does indeed keep gloomy thoughts at bay.'

'Is Frank your son, Sir?' I ask.

'No, we bear no kinship. And yet,' he pauses, 'he is more than a son to me, though I pay him a servant's wage. The good lord saw fit to deliver him to my household after Tetty died. Frank is black and I, as you can plainly see, am white. Time and circumstance can be cruel; the enslavement of black people in the colonies is rife and even here in London some villains choose to practise it, but I offer Frank a safe haven.'

'As you do many others,' says Anon.

Oh my Chrono! That must be the real reason Kwesi didn't want us to leap to 1752. I know about slavery but thought it only happened in the Caribbean and America. Not in Britain. And maybe that's why that couple were staring so hard at me earlier – they wanted to BUY me. I could be in terrible danger! I take deep breaths and remind myself how lucky I am to be in Mr Johnson's house. A safe haven. His face twitches into a smile.

'Frank has a greater claim on me than the others. He has

barely reached his first decade. And he is particularly obsessed with the sea and the change in the calendar this September.' He stands, walks across the room and opens a long thin cupboard to the right of the fireplace. 'It is my good fortune that you are here today. I require your opinion.'

He takes a brown paper package out of the cupboard, places it on the table and unwraps it. I almost gasp out loud.

It's a large hourglass, as high as a relay baton with dark wood bases at each end, connected by three columns. It's an Infinity-Glass without the infinity symbols! It must be THE Infinity-Glass!

'This is a present for Frank. He is obsessed with time and the sea, though this wicked time dictated he was born into slavery and the sea is an unhallowed graveyard for blacks. What say ye?'

'It is exquisite,' says Anon. 'And we must fight against these crimes of commerce!'

Big Ben and I nod in agreement. We're both moved by Mr Johnson's speech, his kindness to Frank and his anger against slavery. And we're too amazed by the coincidence to speak. So much to take in.

'You must not breathe a word of this. It must be a surprise. Tomorrow, before noon, Frank will break his fast with this.'

There's a sharp knock on the door panel. Mr Johnson clumsily attempts to cover up the hourglass and says in his loud voice:

'Come in. What is it, Mistress Anna?'

'Will you be dining with your . . .' she looks at the hourglass and frowns at us '. . . friends this evening and is Master Francis—?'

'No, Mistress Anna. I shall be dining with you alone.'

Mistress Anna smiles and leaves the room. Is it my imagination or did Anon jump when he said alone? I bet Anon wishes she lived here instead of Mistress Anna. Their names are so similar, Mistress Anna could almost be a Leapling herself! She's not, though, Anon would have told us if she was. But something else grabbed me more: the word Francis. I take a deep breath like I'm about to run the 100 metres. My heart is thumping in my chest but I can't let this opportunity slip by. I have to be absolutely sure what I'm thinking is true.

'Who's Master Francis?'

'Why, Frank, dear girl. Mistress Anna insists on using his baptismal name but the rest of us truncate it.'

Anon has risen from her seat. 'We really must take our leave, Mr Johnson. Thank you for your hospitality.'

'The pleasure was mine.'

Everyone stands. He kisses Anon on the hand and waves at Big Ben and me. We wave back. I'm so excited I can barely walk back down the spiral staircase.

It can't be coincidence. The Francis about to receive an hourglass as a present must be Francis 1752. What are the odds on this happening? Even Big Ben won't be able to work it out!

∞ Chapter 11:00 ∞

THE LITTERATI

As soon as we leap back to the Clashroom in 2021, I have lots of thoughts at the same time, buzzing round my head like bees.

As the past is fixed, what just happened in 1752 actually happened in history.

That makes us the first people to know Mr Johnson bought the Infinity-Glass as a present for Francis!

Who carved the infinity symbols into it, when did they do it and why?

We must visit Francis as soon as we possibly can!

But as I'm a Level 1 Infinite on a mission, I need to be careful what I say and who I say it to. I like Anon but she's Evil Nine's sister. More importantly, this school has cameras which record sound as well as visuals. If I say the wrong thing, it could jeopardise our goal to get the Infinity-Glass back to the museum and prove MC^2 is innocent.

So what I actually say is this: 'Is Mr Johnson autistic?'

Anon smiles. 'No, he is not. He may appear to be stimming when he waves his hand or makes noises, but this does not calm him or give him joy as it does us. And he derives intense pleasure from conversing with visitors morning, noon and night which I, for one, could never endure.'

Big Ben nods. 'Logical.'

I frown. 'If he's not autistic, what is he?'

'Dear Samuel probably has Tourette's Syndrome but he does not know it by that name. In 1752 it had not been discovered. It means he cannot control his repetitive movements and vocalisations. His supreme intellect and extreme challenge spring from the same source. The ignorant mock him; intellectuals flock to him.'

'I LIKE him.'

'I too, child. His compassion is embodied in the marine sandglass he bought to comfort young Frank on the morrow. And I like you and Big Ben, too.' Anon twiddles her glasses. 'But now I need solitude. The transition back to the 21st century is always an assault on the senses. My phone number is 1709, dear Samuel's birth year. Text me if you wish to stay in touch.

'Go, Intercalaries! Change your clothes but retain your new outfits. They may be of use in the past should you wish to revisit. And make haste. Anno awaits you in the Art Department on the first floor.'

We leave. I understand exactly why Anon finds it difficult going from one century to another. I'm actually relieved to be back in 2021. It was very noisy and smelly in 1752 and although I loved everyone speaking like Shakespeare, my head hurts from having to concentrate so much. But it's different for Anon: her specialist subjects are poetry AND Mr Johnson. 1752 is her favourite year.

∞

I desperately want to talk with Big Ben about Francis and the Infinity-Glass but there are cameras at every angle of the corridor and up the stairs so it will have to wait. The Art Department is clearly marked. We're about to knock on the door when it opens and Anno beckons us inside.

'I hope you enjoyed your trip to Mr Johnson's house,' she says. 'Anon's heart is 18th century but I prefer the 21st. Welcome to our fundraising project, Planet Plastic!'

I blink. Before my eyes is a massive rectangular room like an art gallery but there's nothing on the whitewashed walls. Instead, there are larger-than-life-sized sculptures made of wire, mangled plastic bottles and sweet wrappers. Some of them are on pedestals and others are hanging from strings like mobiles and constantly moving. They're all modelled on people: jumping, throwing, running. Athletes!

'Wow!' I say.

'I thought you might appreciate these, Elle. They were begun last year for the 2020 Olympic Games that never took place. I became interested in non-events in leap years, discarded things. This exhibition's called On Your Marks, Set, Gone!'

Big Ben and I smile at the wordplay.

'So you're telling a story with art?'

'Yes,' Anno says.

I notice a sculpture in the corner that looks like it's doing the high jump, taking off from the left leg made of grey metal sheets; the right leg hasn't been made yet.

'Is that like prosthetic limbs?' I say.

'Yes. We're working on the Paralympics next.'

'Who's we?'

Anno gestures for us to sit down on a couple of wooden chairs that have dried yellow paint on them. When I make a face, she shrugs her shoulders.

'My daughter, Portia, whom you've met. And local students who aren't scared to get their hands dirty. They called the project Planet Plastic. The primary materials are junk, rubbish, litter. Non-recyclable stuff that would end up in landfill.'

'But you recycle it into art?'

'We do. In fact, I have a private view this Saturday at the Museum of the Past, the Present and the Future. Would you and Big Ben like to attend? It would be wonderful if you could read your poem. I regret you never had the chance to share it on Monday.'

I've never been to an art exhibition before but I like Anno's sculptures and I DEFINITELY want to read my poem.

'Yes. Please.'

'And you, Ben?'

Big Ben pauses before he answers. 'Yes.'

∞

Big Ben and I get changed early for the athletics meeting so we have a chance to catch up properly outside the building but away

105

from the athletics stadium. Even here, we have to be careful about hidden cameras. We must text Francis; we can't ask him about the Infinity-Glass directly in case we spoil the surprise. But we CAN request to meet him the day he receives it, the 24th of June. Mr Johnson said he was giving it to Francis in the morning so we could ask to meet him in the afternoon. Big Ben decides it's best to let Francis know we've already visited 1752.

We met Mr Johnson for tea. Sorry we missed you!

Can we visit you 24 June at 2?

Where can we meet?

'Can you think of anything else?' I say.

'No. He's ten. Keep it simple. Elle . . .'

'What's wrong, BB?' I press send.

'We wasted time today. We should leap to The Vicious Circle and find the ancient Glass.'

'But we don't know where The Vicious Circle is. They only tell adults when they take their children there to swear the Oath. I could ask Grandma, I guess. You could ask your mum. But the Infinity-Glass might not be there any more. It could be anywhere!'

'Can you remember any clues in the room? Were there papers?'

It's a good point. If I'd seen some paperwork, it might have revealed an address. But I didn't see any.

'Even if we find the Infinity-Glass, MC^2 could still get a prison sentence, BB. We have to prove he DIDN'T steal it.'

'Maybe he did. Maybe they have proof that he did so he's in prison.'

I sigh. 'I still think we did well today. We went to 1752—'

'We ate cake.' Big Ben rarely interrupts me. I can tell he's frustrated. 'We didn't meet Francis.'

'We will. We must. Francis might . . . BB, my Chronophone's buzzing!'

Even though there's nobody else outside with us, I still look around to make sure. I try to stay calm but my heart is pounding in my chest. I don't get many messages so it has to be . . . it IS. A message back from Francis!

Meet me at the front of the Cathedral of St Paul in London on the 24th day of June 1752, at 2 of the clock.

Brilliant! We're meeting Francis straight after he's received the Glass. We're one step closer to solving the crime.

∞ Chapter 12:00 ∞

12 SECONDS DEAD

The athletics stadium looks even better in the early evening light, with groups of teenagers limbering up in their bright sports clothes. On the back straight I see a mixed-race girl with two ginger plaits do a three-point-start and sprint 30 metres. She's wearing a yellow running vest with a number 3 pinned to the front and back. Ama! I want to sprint across the grass to greet her but it's forbidden since the throwers have started their warm-ups. I jog round, enjoying the feel of the bouncy track in my borrowed trainers.

'Ama!'

She turns her head and gives me her gap-toothed grin. 'Elle!'

We hug. I only usually let Grandma or Big Ben hug me because they hug hard but these are exceptional circumstances. I haven't seen Ama since last year. My mouth starts speaking before my brain's had time to process my excitement.

'What are you signed up for? Have you seen Kwesi recently? Did he tell you about MC²?'

'One thing at a time, sis,' she says and we both start gently jogging, remembering we need to warm up our bodies not our tongues. 'I'm down for the 100 metres and long jump. What about you?'

'The same. Anno said we're in the same heat for the sprint. She knows I want to race you, even though you're Under 17s and I'm Under 15s. We won't be in the same race if we make the finals, though.'

'Wreckage!' says Ama, which means she thinks it's great. 'What's your PB now, Elle? Wasn't it 13.12 last year? Gone under 13 seconds yet?'

'12.79,' I say. 'What about you?'

'12 seconds dead!'

My eyes go bigger than Jupiter. 'That's brilliant! Kwesi never told me.'

Ama laughs. 'He's too busy with graffiti and Infinite stuff to talk athletics. I've been training hard with the elites. You should leap to 2049, join our group.'

'I can't decide now, I'm on a case. But maybe when it's—'

We hear a guttural roar from the shot put circle, see the heavy black ball launch into the air like a missile and drop almost outside the pit! There's loud applause. It's a woman athlete, squat with cropped black hair. It can't be. It is. Nona. She's obviously helping the teens warm up and can't resist showing off her skills. She may be Evil Nine but she certainly knows how to put the shot! She leaves the group in the charge of one of the coaches and I see her chatting with a couple of lanky boys, one white with blond hair, the other black with cornrowed hair.

Talking of long-legged boys, Big Ben joins us on our second lap. He's warming up for the 800 metres, which is the first track event. Big Ben's super fit this season because he's been running in football practice as well as athletics but I think he's more interested in the scores than the game. They keep putting him in goal when he'd be better at attacking. I notice Portia jogging behind us, her peacock hair glinting in the sunlight. She catches us up.

'Better than Intercalary International,' she says, meaning the track.

'How do you know?' I say. 'It's not open to outsiders.'

That came out the wrong way. I wish I could be relaxed around Portia.

'I saw a photo online. Secret Leapling website, of course.'

I try to think of something pleasant to say. 'Are you running today?'

'Yes, Elle. I'm doing the 100 metres. I'd normally be Under 20s but there weren't enough of us so they lumped me in with the Veterans. I'm racing Aunt Nona. She'll probably beat me.'

'Really?' I say. 'How fast can you run the 100 metres?'

'14 something. Sprinting's not really my thing. I prefer long distance but it's too hot today. Big Ben's very brave doing the 800.'

What a stupid thing to say. The 800 is middle distance not LONG distance. But thankfully I don't say anything. I just nod.

∞

The Under 15 boys are on the start line for the 800 metres. The starter looks like a teen himself. He's short, wearing a black back-to-front baseball cap and matching shades that contrast with his white skin. His red blazer and white trousers are too formal for his headgear. He holds one orange starting pistol in each hand: one for the start, the other in case there's a false start. He reminds me of someone but I can't think who.

'On your marks,' he says in a loud voice.

He fires the gun, the digital timer starts timing and the 800 metres gets off to a good start. I'm standing on the grass verge opposite the start so I can cheer Big Ben for the final lap. I can sense the excitement in the stadium for the first race. Most spectators are sitting under the shelter beside the home straight. I can just make out Anon, and she gives me a wave. She's cooling herself with a mustard silk fan to match her dress.

I know how Big Ben likes to run this distance: keeping to the back of the pack for the first 400 metres then surging forwards to take the lead down the back straight. There are ten boys in total and I notice the two Nona was speaking to earlier, blond and cornrow, are also keeping to the back. But the pace is slow, too slow for Big Ben, so he's going to have to change tactics. He does. By the time they reach the end of the first lap, the pack has split into two groups of five and Big Ben's at the back of the first group behind blond and cornrow.

The bell jangles to mark the final lap!

There's a sudden increase in pace round the bend and as they approach the back straight, Big Ben moves to an outer lane to overtake cornrow but cornrow also moves further out, like he's blocking. Big Ben sees the gap between blond on the inside, cornrow on the outside and accelerates to overtake between them. But as he does, both of them close the gap and jostle Big Ben hard. He falls to the ground. I gasp. He's out of the race! The second pack are catching up.

But Big Ben gets up immediately and begins running faster and faster until he's again at the back of the front pack. And he doesn't stop there. He goes super wide round the bend, overtaking blond, till he's level with cornrow inside him, then moves into third place. Before cornrow can respond, Big Ben continues to accelerate up the home straight, inching towards the boy in second place. He doesn't quite make it and finishes third but the stadium goes crazy. It's only then that I realise I've been shouting ever since he got up from his fall. My throat is sore from cheering him on.

Big Ben's lying down on the track, getting his breath back. His right knee is badly grazed where he fell and he's also been spiked. But I can see he's happy.

'2 minutes 10.437102943,' he says, consulting his stopwatch.

'You did good,' I say.

I don't want to spoil his moment by saying he might have won if he hadn't been jostled. I look across the track to see his two rivals looking over. I give them the cat's eye and they look away. I KNOW it was deliberate but I can't prove it. What good did it do them? The losers lost, as they deserved.

∞

'Elle Ifiè, number 12, lane 1; Mandy Jones, number 7, lane 2 . . .'

The official's reading out our lane draws for the 100 metres. My heart sinks. I HATE lane 1. It's the inside lane next to the field events and I always find it distracting. It's not so much the shouting when someone throws, it's the green of the grass, the constant movement out of the corner of my eye. Your senses are heightened before a race and mine often go into overdrive. Panic begins to rise and my mouth goes dry. Ama comes over to me.

'What's up, sis?'

'I hate lane 1.'

'Then swap with me. I'm in lane 6.'

'It's against the rules!'

'It's not the Olympics. They're scoring by vest numbers, not lanes.'

I'm not sure what to do. I WANT to swap; it seems so easy. But anxiety roots me to the spot; pre-race nerves mixed with the bad lane draw make it hard to think clearly. Ama shrugs.

'Up to you. You got ten minutes to make up your mind. But let me know. I don't want to nail my blocks in the wrong lane.'

At that precise moment, there's a massive cheer from the high jump. Maria just cleared 1 metre 60! I'm pleased for Maria, it's a PB for her, and it's helped me make my decision. I'll definitely be better off in lane 6, away from the field events. I tell Ama and she gives me the thumbs up.

∞

The whistle blows and the starter takes his place by the 100-metre start line.

'On your marks . . .'

I leap into the air, walk forwards and settle down onto the track, placing my feet in the blocks and my hands just behind the white line.

'Set . . .'

I slowly raise my body and lean back against the blocks, my heart pounding in my chest.

BANG! My reaction time's good! I drive out of the blocks like my life depends on it and pound down the track. Around 30 metres I'm upright and in my stride. I relax. I'm totally in the zone, my body and mind in the moment, and all that matters is the bright orange track and the two white lines that are lane 6. That's the best thing about running: the world slips away. I'm focused, I'm fast and I'm finishing. I dip at the line, suddenly aware of a movement on my left. Someone else got there first. Ama? She should easily have won since her PB's almost three quarters of a second faster than mine. I decelerate round the bend and turn round to see how Ama did.

That's when I realise something's wrong.

Several girls are walking off the track post-race but no Ama. I look back down to the start and see her, lying on the ground in lane 1. Poor Ama! She must have pulled a muscle at the start. That's rare. You usually get injuries mid-race from straining too much. I run back down the track, even though you're not supposed to. I have to help my friend.

By the time I get there, one or two officials have beaten me to it. Ama's face is screwed up into a ball, like she's old and wrinkly. She's obviously in agony. She's holding her left calf.

'Ama,' I say, 'don't move. They'll get a stretcher.'

'I've been shot!' she says.

'What? There's no blood.'

She doesn't answer. The officials are frowning. Then the truth hits me like a punch in the stomach. Ama would know if it was a pulled muscle. They happen all the time to athletes. When the starter fired the starting gun, he must have fired at lane 1 at the same time. Not to kill but to hurt. Ama and I swapped lanes. That shot was meant for me!

Everything seems to happen in slow motion after that. Big Ben's by my side and starts stimming because he's so upset by what just happened but I don't think he knows all the details yet. He was looking forward to our race as much as I was. The stretcher arrives, a person in a white coat appears out of nowhere and Ama is taken away. I start following the stretcher when, out of the corner of my eye, I see a small figure in a red blazer disappearing behind the main school building. I make my decision. Ama's in safe hands. We need to stop the gunman!

'BB,' I say, 'Ama's been shot. The gunman went that way. Come on!'

He stops stimming.

'Too dangerous!'

'He's behind the school building.'

'He could shoot us too.'

'He COULD but . . . I think he's escaped by leaping. Something tells me . . . BB, I need to go somewhere quiet.'

Big Ben understands immediately. Everything's happened so quickly on top of the adrenaline of a race and it's too much for me to process. If I don't get to a quiet place, I'll go into shutdown. But the only quiet space we can think of, where no one will disturb us, is the other side of the school building.

By the time we've walked to the quiet space, I feel much calmer. But as soon as we get there, I realise I've made a big mistake. For a split second, we're alone. Then, in front of the school entrance, the faint outline of a short figure in a cap and blazer comes into view. The gunman obviously leapt away after the shooting but is leaping back now to finish the job. At exactly the same time, out of nowhere, a red sports car screeches to a halt in front of us and the gunman's forced to dive sideways to avoid getting run over! It's the Lamborghini, the same car that tried to kill US! The driver winds down the window and the back doors spring open.

'Get in the car. Now!' says a familiar voice.

I look at Big Ben; Big Ben looks at me. We've got one second to make a decision. Refuse to enter the car that almost killed us two days ago and face the gunman, unarmed; or get in the car and risk a totally unknown fate.

We get in the car.

'Fasten your seatbelts,' says Portia. 'Flight-time!'

∞ Chapter 13:00 ∞

PORTIA

No time to process what's happening. No time for what-big-eyes. Big Ben and I clunk-click our belts on the two back seats while the car turns left out of the school entrance and down the main road. Portia has one hand on the wheel; the other is furiously tapping into the dashboard. I look at the screen:

MMM School: Wednesday 23 June 2049: 20:02

Same place, same date and same time we left but 28 years ahead.

'Is this your car? Why are we leaping? What's happening?' I say.

'Hold on,' she says. 'I need to concentrate on take-off.'

The main road's empty. One minute we're going at normal speed, the next, the car makes a roaring sound, my back's glued to the seat then a jolt, and the wheels leave the ground! Big Ben punches the air but I feel like I left my stomach behind on the tarmac and my heart's in danger of jumping out of my chest onto the empty front seat. I'm scared to speak in case I throw up. It

117

takes us about a minute before we level up. The clouds are wispy and beautiful against the pale blue sky but I wish I was on the ground.

'OK. Guess you need an explanation,' says Portia. She runs her fingers through her peacock hair so it goes all spiky again.

'What is it?' says Big Ben, meaning the car, but Portia ignores him.

'You're both in lots of danger. My advice? Back off.'

'This is better than Season's Ferrari. Can I land it?'

'BB, we have to listen.' My voice sounds all whispery but I force the words out. I wish I didn't feel so sick. 'Back off from what?'

'Don't play stupid, Elle. And don't play games with the bad guys.'

'We're not playing games,' I say.

'Then how come you delivered the Infinity-Glass to The Vicious Circle? You want to work for them? No? Didn't think so. You know too much and you know what happens to kids who know too much?'

'They exit them?'

'Look. I know you're after the reward but it's not worth—'

'What reward?' says Big Ben.

'£10,000. The museum's desperate to get the Glass back. It's priceless. And the police aren't likely to find it. Millennia's paying off half the police force.'

'That's a lot of money,' says Big Ben.

But I'm only half listening. She didn't answer my question; she changed the subject. DO they exit kids who know too much?

118

No answer is scarier than a yes. What could be worse than being killed?

'We're about to reach 2049. Safer than 2021.'

The car violently swerves and I put my hand over my mouth.

'Sorry about that. Has a mind of its own.'

'Driverless mode needs reprogramming,' says Big Ben.

I don't really need to hear that at this point in time.

'What happens to kids who know too much?' I say.

Portia sighs. 'What happened to me. I have to work for The Vicious Circle. For life!'

∞

Landing is thankfully smooth. But I still projectile vomit onto the back of the front seat. Portia isn't bothered. She presses a button and the seat starts oozing with foam.

'Self-washing,' she says. 'You OK?'

I nod. It's not strictly true but I don't want to draw too much attention to myself. Here we are in front of the Triple M School in 2049. It's quiet and none of the lights are on. Obviously, no one's around. But I still can't relax, expecting to see the gunman appear out of thin air any moment. Portia sees me looking.

'Don't worry, our trigger-happy friend won't find us here. He dislikes our near future. That's why I chose 2049.'

'How do you know?'

'The Grandfather was born in the 19th century, prefers the 20th and wreaks havoc in the 21st. He helped Millennia turn The Oath Keepers into The Vicious Circle by exiting her enemies

119

one by one. Some say he's the real criminal mastermind, not her. Spent his teens leaping from the 19th century to the 21st. But you probably worked that out already.'

I hadn't, actually. The athletics meeting was so absorbing with the boys trying to mess up Big Ben in the 800 metres, my own race and Ama's shooting. I knew there was something familiar about the gunman but didn't put two and two together. I must be careful I don't let my athletics passion get in the way of solving this crime. But useful to know The Vicious Circle used to be The Oath Keepers.

'Why do you call him The Grandfather when he's only a boy?'

'You really don't know?' She sits down on the school steps. 'He's MILLENNIA's grandfather, on her mother's side. Comes from a long line of watchmakers. Heard of grandfather clocks? He could make one single-handed!'

I smile at the wordplay. Why do baddies have the best names? But I'm still puzzled.

'If he's Millennia's grandfather, how come he's not old or dead?'

'He IS dead. He died as an old man in 1925. But this is the 3-leap +1 version of him. He simply leaps from the 19th century into his future, which is our present, then leaps back. Don't you have any friends from times past?'

I think of Francis texting us from 1752 and nod. He's a virtual friend; we haven't met him in person yet. But we will soon, I hope.

I decide to join Portia sitting on the school steps as I still feel quite shaky but Big Ben remains standing. I can tell he's unhappy about something. He draws his eyebrows right down to his eyes at Portia.

'It was you driving,' he says.

'I wasn't going to let you land in a million—'

'Not today. Summer solstice. You tried to run us over!' Portia shrugs but doesn't say anything and Big Ben finishes. 'I see how you landed the Lamborghini so brilliant. It was you.'

Portia sighs. 'OK, Sherlock. I won't lie to you, it WAS me. And this is a Lamborghini Quarto Millennio. So what? Think I'd risk everything to save you now if I tried to kill you two nights ago? I was SENT to kill you, once we worked out Elle witnessed the Circle meeting. The thief admitted someone snatched the glass off them; everyone knew you were at the museum to recite your Infinity-Glass poem, Elle; and you're the only one who can leap to a nanosecond. It had to be you. But I deliberately messed up the hit. I wasn't going to run down a couple of kids.'

Big Ben waits several seconds before he nods. 'Logical.'

'I filmed the hit for Millennia. It looks like your brilliant reflexes saved you rather than my brilliant driving! Hoped it would scare you off. Obviously, I was wrong.'

I frown at her. 'Will they kill you for saving us now?'

'Probably not. They'll come up with a punishment worse than death. Apprentice me to Aunt Nona.' She laughs. 'They won't get rid of me; I'm family. Besides, I'm too good.'

'At driving?'

'Yes. At driving. When mum called me Portia, she thought Shakespeare not Top Gear. But my skills come in handy.'

'Are we going to stay here all night?'

'No. We need to collect Ama from hospital. Drive her home.'

'How do you know she's not badly hurt?'

'Aunt Nona texted.' She sees me stiffen. 'I know she's not your favourite person but she knows about wounds. Even she felt bad when Ama got shot instead of you. Come on! Haven't got all night.'

∞

We reach the hospital just after Ama's been discharged. She's sitting in the reception with Kwesi and GMT who look far more worried than she does. She gives me one of her gap-toothed smiles.

'I'll beat you next time, sis!'

'I'm sorry, Ama.' I almost whisper the next bit. 'That bullet was meant for me.'

'I know,' she says. 'Kwesi worked it out. Glad it was only a plastic bullet! They wanted to contact my next of kin and I thought Mum and Dad would freak hearing I was injured and where I was, so I texted big bro.

'Anyway,' she continues, 'it's me who should apologise. I never thanked you last year for saving Kwesi. Thanks so much, Elle!'

She hugs me again and I go bright red. I find it difficult getting emotional in front of everyone. I want to hide my face in my hands but that would be even more embarrassing. It's nice Ama thanked me, though.

'I can't take all the credit,' I say. 'I worked in a team.'

By team I mean The Infinites but I can't say that in front of Portia and the nurses because it's top secret. Portia jangles the car keys in her pocket.

'I could stay here all evening listening to the mutual appreciation society,' she smiles so we know she's not being unkind, 'but someone needs to get home.'

∞

Big Ben, Kwesi, GMT and I walk back through town. We were supposed to have our meeting tonight and definitely have some serious catching up to do. It's a warm evening; why risk leaping and possibly being seen by an Annual when we can stroll? Big Ben and I tell them everything about the day: Nona being Evil Nine; Big Ben's meltdown; tea with Mr Johnson and Frank being Francis; the athletics meeting; and Portia. Their eyes get bigger and bigger with each piece of news. Finally, we show them all the Francis texts. It's the first time they know I worked out what France is 1752 meant and contacted Francis.

That last piece of news bothers Kwesi. He frowns so deep he looks 100. He shows us his infinity tattoo on his left hand, bumps fists with us each twice and disappears and reappears on the spot. We gasp. We thought only MC^2 could body blink. GMT translates but we've already worked it out.

'Kwesi says we gotta stay true to the symbol. Gotta look out for each other. Gotta visit MC before we do anything else!'

Kwesi raises his eyebrows at us.

Big Ben nods.

GMT smiles.

'OK,' I say. 'Let's visit MC^2 tomorrow after school. We can't let The Vicious Circle win!'

∞ Chapter 14:00 ∞

PRIME SUSPECT

'Thing is, even if Leaps locate the Glass, peeps'll still say I'm prime.'

It's Thursday after school. MC² has been talking ever since we arrived. Actually, he hasn't stopped talking since we updated him about everything, especially making contact with Francis. This makes me happy. It was scary when he wasn't himself.

We've been allowed to meet him in the main room this time, rather than behind bars. It's a different warden as well, a younger, red-headed man called Bonzo, who's given him more privileges. Although we're sitting on the hard prison chairs, MC² is walking up and down all over the room. Every few seconds he tenses his body like he's about to do the long jump but nothing happens. That explains why he was so exhausted at our last visit. He was overwhelmed after being arrested and had overdone trying to body blink with no success.

Big Ben perks up at the word prime.

'2, 3, 5, 7 and 11. Five of The Vicious Circle are prime numbers.'

'You speak sense,' says MC², 'but I meant prime as in suspect. The one most likely did the crime in a whodunnit. In this case, The Squared. They think I did it cos I messed up in the past. But you got me thinking, BB. Is the Glass still at Vicious Circle HQ or hidden someplace?'

I frown. 'We don't know where The Vicious Circle's headquarters are. If we did, we could try to get it back.'

'I do. Went a coupla times in my Time Squad days. Course, it was Oath Keepers then. GMT's got it on her Chrono.' He pauses. 'I want more on The Vicious Circle. Who's the Three dude again?'

'Mr Oily Hair,' I say. 'He knew the thief. He told Millennia they were family. He kept talking about his sister and . . . oh my Chrono! He said, "Show some respect, Nine. You're letting down the family." Mr Oily Hair must be Nona's brother.'

'Family could mean crime ring. That's how crims speak, sis.'

'I know. But now I remember, they LOOK like they could be the same family. They both have short black hair and look like shot putters. Evil Nine IS a shot putter!'

'Logical,' says Big Ben. '11's a prime number. Is 11 their grandfather?'

'No, BB. He's Millennia's grandfather.' I pause. No wonder Big Ben didn't take in everything Portia said. So much happened that evening; I'm still processing it myself. 'I have an idea. If Mr Oily Hair is Nona's brother then he's also Anno and Anon's brother. When he said the thief was family, he must have meant one of those two.'

MC^2 stops walking. 'So, the thief was Anno or Anon?'

'Yes! But I can't believe it. They're both so nice.' I remember Anon taking us to Mr Johnson's house and Anno inviting me to read my poem this Saturday at her private view. But they're both the same height as me and a similar athletic build. Maybe it WAS one of them.

'No!' Big Ben is shaking his head. 'Anno or Anon or MC^2 . . .'

'Me?' MC^2 freezes.

'You can't be serious,' says GMT. She turns to MC^2. 'I told them it was me stole the watches, not you. They can't believe—'

'. . . Or Elle,' says Big Ben.

'Me?' I say.

'It has to be someone the same size as Elle.'

'That makes sense. But if it was me, I'd have leapt back in time TWICE. There'd be THREE of me: one on the school trip; one stealing the Glass; and the other trying to stop the thief.' I stand up. 'Of course I wasn't the thief, BB. I'd never steal and I'm not family.'

'Me neither, bruv.' MC^2 gives Big Ben the cat's eye. 'Nice try.'

'I have another idea.' Everyone looks at me then looks away. 'Portia. She's the same size as me.'

'No,' says Big Ben. 'She saved us from the gunman.'

'Not logical. She still could have been the thief.' I frown at Big Ben. Is he letting his feelings for Portia cloud his judgement? I try to ignore my own feelings of jealousy and continue talking. 'So prime suspect for the theft is either Anno or Anon or Portia.'

Big Ben's shaking his head again. 'Anon walks with a stick, so how can she leap and try to fight you, Elle?'

127

'Good point, BB. But remember she used to be a gymnast. She leaps to 1752 on her own to see Mr Johnson. Old people can be strong and fit so she's still a prime suspect.' I pause. 'If her sister Anno did it, she would have had to leap from the past or the future to commit the crime, since she was also giving the talk about the Infinity-Glass. And one of them is probably the missing Eight. They missed the meeting because they were committing the crime.'

'Good work, sis. But where's your proof?' MC^2 sighs.

The warden clears his throat and MC^2 brightens up.

'Listen up, Leaps! I forgot to give Bonzo a befitting intro. He's a keeper of the keys who'll never set me FREE but he loves the 4/4, TOO.'

I frown. MC^2 speaking in rhyme always gives me a headache, though I like his wordplay. But his emphasis was odd. Either he's losing his touch or . . . he's speaking in code again! FREE 4/4 TOO. 3442. That must be Bonzo's telephone number! Which means he's a Leapling or an Annual with a Chronophone who's been trained how to use it and MC^2 wants us to have his number. I make a mental note of it, wishing MC^2 would be more direct.

'He's into hip hop?' I say, keeping my voice steady.

'Yeah. Fan of mine and Einstein. We're NUMBER one on his chart.'

Bonzo gives a fake bow and out of the corner of my eye, I see it. A tiny flicker, a brief outline of MC^2 before he appears solid again. I don't think anyone else noticed and if you saw it on the CCTV, you'd think it was a technical glitch. I narrow my eyes at him; he winks at me. That confirms it. MC² has somehow managed to body blink in Do-Time, in spite of the Anti-Leap. And if he's able to body blink, the next step is a full-on leap!

∞

For the second half of the visit, we discuss Francis.

'Kwesi, I know we sparred over this but I gotta get out of this spit. Give Leaps the lowdown on Francis.'

Kwesi frowns but MC² keeps talking.

'Me and Kwesi met Francis May Day, 1752. Brother's an Annual but he thought my Chronophone the best thing since green tea so we gave him one, taught him how to use it. I know it's breaking the Oath, but Francis was lonesome. A boy of ten won't harm nothing. He learnt quick; most Annuals take years. Francis said his master knows everyone in London, upper crust to crims. Peeps drop by morning, noon and night. This woman used to follow Francis when he left the house. Asked lots of questions. Said she was writing an article about timepieces. Francis knew nothing. He hadn't bin given the Glass yet, I guess. I thought nothing at the time but since I got arrested, it clicked. There must be a clue back in the day. Only way to find out is leap.'

Kwesi's shaking his head like he's got a swarm of bees in it. He signs for a full minute before MC² translates.

'Brother says he don't want you meeting Francis in no 1752. The present's the devil you know but the deep past is the devil for real. Nothing's the same. Peeps eat, sleep and speak different.

It's a noisy, smelly Armageddon for autistic folks. Worst is, black people are slaves; Francis still gotta buy his freedom. You wanna meet Francis, meet him virtual on your Chronophone.'

It's what I thought. Kwesi chose not to explain France is 1752 was Francis 1752 because of slavery. But if Francis is a slave, how come he lives with Mr Johnson and how did he manage to make friends with MC^2 and Kwesi?

'Kwesi, it's nice you want to keep us safe. But we've already met Francis on the Chronophone. And we've already visited 1752. It was noisy and smelly and I DID find it hard but how could they make me a slave? I could always leap away and escape.' My heart's thumping in my chest; I sound more confident than I feel.

Kwesi wrinkles his mouth like Grandma does when the yam's too bitter. I understand his disgust. Slavery was a terrible thing, especially when people were transported away from their original culture. It was worse than prison: you could be bought and sold to the highest bidder like an object.

Big Ben frowns like he's thinking hard.

'We can't do it by phone. Francis can't send us evidence.'

'I asked him to text me photos of anything suspicious,' MC^2 pauses, 'but he ain't sent nothing. Course, he coulda sent something to me now but Do-Time's got my phone.'

I nod. They took our phones and bags again on this visit. I make a mental note to add Bonzo's phone number as soon as we get our phones back. Big Ben continues.

'Kwesi's logical. Elle can't leap. I can.'

'What?'

'You got danger from The Vicious Circle plus danger from slave owners. One too much danger.'

'BB, I'm not letting you go alone. I contacted Francis; I need to speak to him. I'm going to leap because there's no other way to get the evidence to free MC^2.' I turn to the others. 'Anyone else coming?'

Kwesi shakes his head. MC^2 tenses like he's about to leap out of Do-Time this second. GMT shakes her head at him to say stop that and smiles at us.

'I guess you guys got a plus one. I'm classed as an adult so you got backup if things go wrong. I never visited 1752. I hate it like Kwesi but someone's gotta keep an eye. It's 5 o'clock now. Let's get outta here and leap, guys!'

'Thanks,' I say. 'I've got a funny feeling in my tummy. We're seeing Francis the day he receives the Glass. We might not be his only visitors. The woman who's been pestering Francis might be—'

'The prime suspect,' says MC^2.

∞ Chapter 15:00 ∞

FRANCIS

We leap to an alley near St Paul's Cathedral so we're less likely to be seen appearing out of thin air. Big Ben and I are wearing the 18th-century clothes from yesterday, except I have trainers under the long skirt; GMT's dressed like a boy, her hair scraped into a ponytail, wearing a bottle-green velvet jacket from the 1960s and makeshift breeches. We approach the massive building in awe. The cathedral still looks new because it was totally rebuilt after it burnt down in the Great Fire of London in 1666. I went on a school trip in my primary school so I know where the entrance is.

There are lots of people gathered outside, the men wearing strange white wigs and three-cornered hats; the women in full-length embroidered dresses and silk shoes. The air smells of rotten potatoes and horse poo. At the top of the entrance steps, a small black boy wearing a brown velvet coat, black breeches and black shoes with silver buckles waves at us. Francis! He looks younger than ten but his voice sounds older.

'Greetings, Leaplings!' He gives a little bow. 'Welcome to 1752. Today is the 24th of June but I am sure your Chronophones will inform you of that! Did you have a good trip? Are you coming back for the 11-day leap and the Carnival of the Calendar? The Master procured me a ticket for he knows everyone in London but he knows not of the existence of Leaplings.'

'Good to meet you, honeybee,' says GMT, bowing back. 'Hey, we only just got here. One trip at a time.'

Francis laughs. 'You must be GMT in men's attire. And you must be Elle and you must be Big Ben. And I am merely Master Francis.'

'I like your name,' I say.

'So do I. It is still fresh on my lips from the christening. It is not the name I was enslaved with.'

'What were you called before?'

Francis beckons us to follow him and we walk down the steps and turn left.

'I was alone at the May Day celebration, amid much dancing and merriment, when a voice said, "Quashey!" I replied, "Yes," for that was my previous name. I turned around to see two young men, black as me, wearing curious attire, and I was puzzled since I knew them not. And they were puzzled too since it was the first time they had encountered me.'

'MC^2 and Kwesi!' I say. 'Kwesi and Quashey's the same name.'

'That one word drew us together by chance. Had MC^2 not addressed his friend that very second, we should never have met. I have a good master and splendid lodgings but am surrounded by those who have seen better days. I longed for young company. And now I have it: MC², Kwesi and you.'

'Are you a slave or not?'

That didn't come out how I wanted it to but that's what I really want to know.

'I am servant to Mr Johnson, slave to Colonel Bathurst, my old master. I was born into slavery in Jamaica. When Colonel Bathurst came back to England, he brought me with him. His son, a kind man, looked after me and bestowed me upon Mr Johnson this April. I am still bound to my previous master until I buy my freedom.'

'You have to PAY to be free!' My mouth is a capital O. He should never have been enslaved in the first place. They should pay Francis money.

'I do. But Mr Johnson pays me a small sum so one day I'll have enough money. But I never discuss it; the Master turns purple with rage at the very word slavery, but his views are considered eccentric.'

'What do you do as a servant?'

'Very little. The most taxing job is tending to Master's wig.'

I try not to laugh: he's not doing a very good job!

'If you have a job, does that mean you don't go to school?'

'I boarded in Yorkshire but now the Master instructs me.'

Big Ben frowns. 'What about your parents? Do they miss you?'

'I have no recollection of them.'

'Me neither,' I say. 'My mum's dead but my dad's alive somewhere in Nigeria. I don't know him. Grandma's like a mum to me.'

'As Mr Johnson is like a father to me. "Family," he declares,

134

"are those who live in the same house."'' He pauses. 'If I were a Leapling, I might leap to Jamaica to discover my family. Or leap to the future where I would no longer be a slave. But I was born an Annual and predestined to live in this century.

'Leaplings, it is 1752 and we are out of doors. The Master says there is no better city than London. It is my duty, therefore, to show you London and your duty to paint the future before my very eyes.'

We turn into a wide, dusty, potholed street and it's like someone has turned the volume and visuals and smells up! The sound of horses' hooves against the cobbles, pulling carriages full of people with powdered faces, the women with beauty spots; steaming horse poo; sheep running riot; people shouting from shop windows like it's an outdoor market; pedestrians with scarred, twisted faces; far more black people than I was expecting, which makes me feel a bit better – they can't all be slaves; tiny ragged children with eyes too big for their heads; the air thick as soup. Breathing through my mouth doesn't help. Francis helps us cross the road.

'I see the past overwhelms you.'

I nod, unable to answer. GMT gives me a concerned look and offers me a sweet. She unwraps it and pops it into my mouth so I don't have to coordinate whilst I'm walking. Orange! This isn't leapsickness, it's sensory overload, but it does the trick. I focus on the flavour and try to make everything else fade into the background.

Thankfully, we take a right turn and it's quieter, though still bustling with shops and people.

'Friday Street,' says Francis proudly, like he named it himself. 'You will appreciate there are fewer carriages in the back streets; they are not built for horses.'

'Do you have cars?' says Big Ben.

'Alas, no!' says Francis. 'MC^2 sent me a video of a Tesla on the Chronophone he gave me. Future vehicles are far superior to now.'

'Cars are noisy and bad for the planet!' says GMT. 'Least you can use manure to grow plants.'

Big Ben's shaking his head. 'Eco-cars are the future. When I invent one.'

Francis does what-big-eyes. 'You invent cars?'

'When I'm grown up.'

'You are already grown!'

We all smile. Big Ben is the tallest person in the street. Pedestrians and shopkeepers do what-big-eyes at his spiky hair and too-short breeches. I try not to think about how much attention he's attracting to us but everyone's staring at Francis, GMT and me just as much. Maybe they're wondering whether Francis is an escaped slave, if GMT's a boy or a girl and what on earth I'm wearing on my feet! It's 1752 and we stand out. No wonder they're staring.

'So, the London of the future is noisier than this?' says Francis.

I nod. 'There are red buses as well as cars, and lots of planes flying overhead and London Underground tube trains and—'

'What are buses and planes and tube trains? Describe them.'

We do our best but it's quite hard describing something that hasn't even been IMAGINED in 1752.

The streets get narrower and narrower, I start to feel claustrophobic and Francis tenses like MC^2 does when he's about to leap.

'What's wrong?'

'Chamber pots!'

'We shoulda brought an umbrella,' says GMT.

I lower my head and hunch like I'm 100. I HATE 1752. It's noisy, dirty and evil. No wonder Kwesi told us not to come. But Big Ben seems to like it. He's impressing Francis about aeroplanes and getting his Chronophone out to send him some videos. They make a strange contrast: Big Ben, super tall, scruffy and white; Francis, well-dressed, small and black. GMT warns them to keep the Chronophones hidden.

'Fear not, GMT. Children are invisible in 1752.'

'Then why were they staring so much on the main street?'

'They stare but they don't see. When MC^2 did his disappearing act, nobody fainted.'

'He did what? Wait till I get back—'

'I thought he was a duppy, a ghost, and ran direct in front of a passing coach but Kwesi secured me. He told me they were Leaplings from the future. I wish I had the power to leap through time!'

'Did Kwesi speak?'

'No. He wrote the words on his Chronophone.'

We're on a main road again that Francis calls Thames Street.

'Francis, where are we going?' I say.

'To the river. Prepare your nose for the stench. But your eyes will be rewarded.'

137

We turn right and the smell hits me first. If I thought it was smelly before, the river is far worse. Like every shop's a fish shop and all the sewage of London meets here. GMT helps me take off my shawl and use it to cover my nose and mouth like a mask. I don't care if I look weird; I just have to hold it together. But a split second later, I forget about the smell.

My mouth forms a capital O.

I see London Bridge and the River Thames but not like I recognise from my primary school trip. London Bridge has BUILDINGS all the way across it on both sides, so many, surely it will collapse with the weight! And the Thames is much, much wider and so full of boats, barges and small ships, I wonder how they have space to sail at all! Francis is staring at the river like it's his specialist subject.

'Here they have frost fairs when the Thames freezes over. I cannot IMAGINE more fun. Tell me,' he says, 'how London has changed between now and the future!'

We approach London Bridge, more like a tunnel with its tall buildings leaning into each other. Most of them are shops with fresh fancy signs outside but the buildings are old and dilapidated. There are crowds of people walking, horses and carriages going both ways, right and left, so we could get run over, and people sitting in covered chairs with poles attached so other people can carry them. I can't believe what I'm seeing.

'Are they disabled?'

'No, they are not. The sedan chair is a common transportation for hire but take note: those adorned with gold and brocade belong to the monied class who wish to be seen but contribute little to society. Master says only their wealth disables them. He ridicules the idle rich.' He pauses. 'Do you wish to cross the bridge to the bankside? Or perhaps we can walk to the new Bridge of Westminster, though we will be obliged to retrace our steps and go via Fleet Street.'

'I'd like to see the new bridge,' I say. 'But can't we cross London Bridge and walk by the river? In the future, you can walk all the way along the South Bank.'

'Alas, there is no path, merely manufactories,' Francis sighs. 'How can I compete with your future? I could show you Tyburn,' he continues, 'but 'tis a long walk and there is no advertised hanging today. Master forbids me to go when there is. But if the villain is famous, we enjoy a public holiday. Do they hang people in London in the future?'

'Goodness, no! But they put them in prison.'

The word prison makes me think of MC^2 and reminds me, as we walk from the river back to Thames Street, that we're not here for sightseeing; we're here on a mission. I want to ask Francis lots of questions but I bite my tongue. We've only just met him; we need to gain his trust. Francis is lonely because he's ten but lives with old people. We must make the day special for him as well as useful for us. It's like he reads my mind.

'I love the river. The Master declares it a lawless sewer, free-flowing or frosted. He fears I might be captured and resold but I have faith I will not. I go there to escape from Mistress Anna when she's angry and watch the boats.'

'We met her yesterday at the house. She was quite grumpy.'

'One day,' says Francis, 'I'm going to sail away on a big ship and travel the world.'

'I want to see the world by Lamborghini Asterion,' says Big Ben.

'Master says a ship is a prison on water, and for many of my fellow brothers it is.' His eyes look serious but then he smiles. 'For me, it will be freedom. Notwithstanding his objections, today Master indulged my passion with a gift. A marine sandglass "to remind you of the sea and the culling of the calendar," he said.'

We stop in our tracks. The background noise of horses and shouting disappears and there's nothing on our minds but the task: quizzing Francis for clues to help get MC^2 out of prison. Yet now Francis has mentioned the sandglass, we're lost for words. As he enjoys talking, he doesn't notice how serious we've all become. We start walking again and Thames Street, with all its sights, sounds and smells, comes back into focus.

'So today is the best day. Having you in my company and receiving the Glass. MC^2 told me Leaplings like 1752 because everyone in England and the colonies leap at the same time. I have spoken often of the 11-day leap since hearing of it, though I never mention Leaplings or The Gift. So much so, the Master is arranging a celebration for me at Gough Square on the 2nd of September. Do say you'll attend.'

'Yes, please!' I say and look at Big Ben.

'OK,' he says.

'Sure,' says GMT.

'The sandglass,' I say, 'did you put it in a safe place?'

'Indeed. It is ensconced in the candle cupboard and only I use it. It is my job to light up the house in the evenings.'

I take a deep breath. 'It's really important you tell us everything you know. MC^2 is in prison and we need your help.'

'I will do all I can to assist.' Francis looks sad. MC^2 is his friend too.

'MC tells us some lady keeps tracking you,' GMT says, wiping sweat off her brow.

'I have not seen her of late.'

'Can you describe her?'

'Tall. Old. She wears spectacles and has a walking stick.'

Oh my Chrono! That sounds like Anon. I suddenly feel sad. I like Anon a lot. I don't want her to be a criminal. But I have to find out more.

'Does she have tea with Mr Johnson?' I say.

'Occasionally. But other times she has approached me in the street. On those occasions, she shows no desire to greet the Master, only an obsession with timepieces.'

'Did you get a photo of her?'

'Alas, no. Kwesi told me to be discreet; the Chronophone must remain hidden. I have not had the opportunity to capture her likeness before she takes her leave.'

'And you definitely haven't seen her today?'

'No. And it is fortunate I have not. For now I have in my possession the marine sandglass she alluded to it would be difficult to deny it.'

'Francis, I know you would hate to tell a lie. I hate lies too. But please don't tell her about your present. Will you promise me?'

'I promise, Elle! But enough of the Glass. Tell me more about the future.'

We walk. We talk. The buildings become cleaner, grander, the women's dresses a little wider and even the horses are better groomed. I start to enjoy 1752, imagining what it would be like to live here until finally, we turn a corner and Francis seems to double in size with pride.

'Behold, Westminster Bridge! And the Palace of Westminster.'

I take in the bright new bridge, and the building we call the Houses of Parliament, and frown. It looks totally different to the one I know, less spiky, more chunky. And there's something else niggling me. It takes a few seconds for it to sink in. Something's missing. There's no tower, no clock, no Big Ben!

∞

When we get back to the house and Francis knocks on the door, we wait at the bottom of the steps. Almost immediately the door flies open and Mistress Anna the housekeeper appears, sweaty and trembling. I'm shocked. She's not angry as I expected – she's scared.

'Master Francis, Master Francis, I am all aghast! That woman, if woman we can call her, has confounded me. My mind is in chaos. I saw her; then I saw her not. Call the surgeon, call the priest. We are bedevilled!'

∞ Chapter 16:00 ∞

BAMBOOZLED

'Madam, I am at your service,' says Francis.

He motions us up the steps. We follow him into the house, pleased Mistress Anna hasn't turned us away but worried about her state of mind. My heart is pounding in my chest. I find it difficult when people act oddly and I don't know them very well. Unpredictable behaviour raises my anxiety levels. I wish there was a grown-up around who could help Mistress Anna calm down. But Mr Johnson and the other occupants of the house are out. Then I remember that GMT's with us, and she's 4 leap +1, 17, so she might know what to do.

Francis guides Mistress Anna into the brown room on the ground floor, where we sat yesterday before we went upstairs to meet Mr Johnson. He gently lowers her into a chair and I'm reminded of The Grandfather helping Millennia take her number 12 seat in The Vicious Circle.

'Friends,' he says, 'watch over her! I must fetch the smelling salts and gin from below. Holler if you need me!'

GMT walks over to Mistress Anna and sits next to her.

'Don't worry, Francis. Mistress Anna's in safe hands.' She lowers her voice a little, 'Ma'am, we apologise for intruding at this difficult time.'

There are a few seconds' silence as Mistress Anna gradually becomes aware that we're here.

'Who are you?'

'GMT, ma'am. And this is Elle, and this is Big Ben. They came to tea yesterday.'

'With that woman!' Mistress Anna goes rigid. 'She has come to haunt me.'

'Did she visit you today?'

Mistress Anna shakes her head. 'It was a visitation.'

'What do you mean?' I say. 'Did she visit you or not?'

I'm glad my voice is gentle but I hope that didn't sound too harsh. It's important we know if it was Anon. Mistress Anna doesn't respond and I bite my tongue. GMT takes over.

'Please tell us what happened in your own time, ma'am.'

Mistress Anna is taking long, deep breaths like I do to centre myself and calm down. The door opens and Francis appears with a tray full of bottles and glasses. He places it on the table, grabs a blue jar, takes out the stopper and waves it under Mistress Anna's nose. Even from here I get the whiff of rotten eggs. She seems to come back to life though her speech is slow.

'She knocked on the door. I answered and told her the Master was out. We have a constant plague of visitors here and a woman needs time to digest a book. She said, "Do you not know who I am? Anon, celebrated poet. It is not the Master I seek today but

Francis" – her very words. I noted her tone was unusually harsh but it is always her habit to announce herself on arrival. I told her to go away since Master Francis was also taking some air. But she forced her stick through the door and said she was happy to wait. She marched into this room and sat in this chair in her fine silk gown as if she were mistress of the house!'

Francis offers Mistress Anna a glass of what must be gin. She takes a sip, splutters like Grandma does when the pepper soup is too spicy, then continues.

'I went back up to my room and became engrossed in my reading. Unfortunately, my hearing is far more acute than my sight. I heard footsteps going upstairs on the first floor so was forced to enquire why she thought fit to explore the building uninvited. "I wish to see the Dictionary," she said. "I have some poetry quotations for Mr Johnson." I hesitated. Why had she not mentioned this upon arrival? But Mistress Anon is obsessed with the Dictionary and some of the scribes were working upstairs. I allowed her access.'

'What happened next, Mistress Anna?' says Francis. I can see he's enjoying being in control rather than her scolding him all the time.

'She was upstairs for some time. Then I heard her descending the stairs. I presumed she was going back down to the parlour before taking her leave, so continued my occupation. My book was particularly compelling and I did not welcome a second interruption. However, she seemed to stop mid-flight, between the first and ground floor, which perplexed me, so I left my room and walked down but two steps to see what had caused her to pause. Madam was standing outside the candle cupboard with a bag on her shoulder I had not noticed previously. I opened my mouth to enquire her business when she . . . she . . . vanished in front of my very eyes! All that remained were glittering scraps, as if she had scattered her own ashes after death!

'Anna, I told myself. You are an educated woman. Apparitions do not exist. I took my broom and discarded the scraps. Then I took to my bed. But when I closed my eyes, the sight of her disappearing haunted me. Were my failing eyes deceiving me or my other senses disarranged? She entered the house but she did not take her leave as mortals do. She disappeared!'

On the word disappeared, Mistress Anna crumples into her chair again, GMT puts the smelling salts under her nose and Francis rushes out of the room and up the stairs. Big Ben and I look at each other, our mouths a capital O. A few seconds later, a strange, strangled cry comes from the landing. Francis! We know what's happened before he comes back downstairs to tell us:

His marine sandglass has been stolen!

∞

Now it's Francis's turn for the smelling salts. He cries so loud the whole of Gough Square must wonder what's going on. His face is covered with tears and snot and I feel sorry for him. I'm reminded that he may speak like he's 20 but he's ten years old and just lost a special present he was only given this morning. No wonder he's upset.

While GMT looks after him, Big Ben and I have work to do. We walk up the first flight of stairs and see the candle cupboard on our right. We look inside. Just candles. Definitely no sandglass. We're about to come back downstairs again when something glinting on the carpet catches my eye. A couple of silver sweet wrappers from leap sweets that Mistress Anna must have missed. This is what she meant by glittering scraps. She wouldn't have recognised it: plastic wasn't invented then.

'Evidence,' I say.

Big Ben nods. 'Only Anon knew Mr Johnson would give the present TODAY. Apart from us. Unless . . .'

'Didn't she mention it when we leapt back to the classroom? She said Mr Johnson was most kind to comfort young Frank.'

'. . . someone played back the footage from the cameras.'

Of course! The Triple M School cameras. Evil Nine, Anno or Portia could easily have replayed our conversation and found out about the date the sandglass would be given to Francis. Anon announced we were going for tea same date, superior location. Maybe she wanted her sisters to know where we were having tea before we left and made sure she gave them information about the sandglass afterwards?

I put the sweet wrappers in my bag and we go back downstairs. Now we have a problem. We don't want to leave Mistress Anna and Francis whilst they're still upset because they might faint like people did in the olden days but we must recover the Glass. It's as if GMT can read my mind.

'You guys go get 'em!' she says, meaning the thief and the thought of it being Anon feels like a punch in the stomach. 'I'll stay and look after these two. I got lots of practice from '68 hangin' out in fields.'

'Thanks,' I say and lower my voice. 'Give us the location for the building and room we took the Oath. The thief must have gone there first! Remember, the Double M offered a reward for a glimpse of the Glass before it had infinity signs.'

GMT smiles. 'I'll text you. You'll have it by the time you reach the alley.'

We're going to leap back via the alley near Mr Johnson's house where we leapt yesterday. Old Meg isn't there this time. Our coast is clear.

'BB,' I say, 'you don't think Mistress Anna stole the Glass and made up the story to lay the blame on Anon? Mistress Anna hates Anon. Maybe it's a trick.'

'Not sure. Leap now, talk later.'

'What time and date?' I say. 'How do we know when the thief leapt back to?'

'We don't,' says Big Ben. 'But we left at 5 o'clock on Thursday the 24th of June; let's leap to 5:01 at The Vicious Circle.'

We check our phones and GMT's text has come through. We have the location for the building and the room. But we need to be even more specific. This is an undercover operation.

'Under the table?' I say.

'Brilliant!' says Big Ben.

We sit opposite each other, link hands and concentrate. Under the table has taken on a totally different meaning. It's not a place of safety; it's high risk. We'll be at the heart of The Vicious Circle!

∞ Chapter 17:00 ∞

THE UNEXPECTED EXITING OF EIGHT

'. . . Regrettable but we must always be prepared for the unexpected,' says Millennia, going into loudspeaker mode.

'No one ever exits The Vicious Circle.' Pause. 'The Vicious Circle exits them.' Evil Nine!

Big Ben and I are under the table, slightly too close to Millennia for my liking but we didn't do a bad job. We're still near the centre. It's very strange being able to see people's legs and shoes. I notice that the teens, One and Two, are wearing futuristic trainers that change colour every few seconds, red, amber and green like traffic lights. They're amazing but I must stop looking in case I get sensory overload. Big Ben clicks the record button on his Chronophone and I give him the thumbs up. We need all the evidence we can get.

'What of the Glass?' Meridian's voice is gravelly as ever yet she sounds more refined than Millennia.

'Which version?' says Mr Oily Hair, aka Three.

'Not this nonentity. It is too new, too perfect. An Anachronism. It does not belong in the present and should never have been stolen from the past.' Meridian pauses. 'I refer, Three, to the aged version of the Infinity-Glass. I assume it has been sold. The Vicious Circle awaits its millions.'

'It is in a safe place, Meridian. My sister—'

'You have too many sisters and I trust none of them.'

She must mean Anno, Anon and Evil Nine.

'Silence!' says Millennia. 'I called this emergency meeting to inform you of the unexpected exiting of Eight, not to discuss museum objects. Eight proposed their departure this afternoon, directly after the procurement of this . . . infinity-free artefact. It has made my year seeing the Glass purchased by the great Dr Johnson prior to its disfigurement. I paid Eight a generous fee and accepted their decision.'

'Did they take the money and run or were they,' Evil Nine clears her throat, 'forced into the decision?'

'You did not consult me!' Meridian has raised her voice.

'I consulted Grandfather.'

'He is not an Elder.'

'Indeed. He is an ANCIENT. That holds more weight.' Pause. 'Does anyone else hold any objections?'

There's silence but a bit of shuffling from One and Two. I do the same. I have lots of experience living under the table from when I was younger but it always made me stiff. Big Ben's decided to lie down on his back and I don't blame him. His head was hard up against the wood. But I hope he doesn't fall asleep and start snoring. That would be a total disaster!

'Then we must act according to protocol,' Millennia continues. 'When a member exits, the remaining members move clockwise to fill the spaces, unless they are under a reprimand or due a promotion. In this case, no one has disgraced themselves; nor has anyone excelled themselves.'

'With respect, esteemed Millennia,' says Three, 'I have time-tabled two thefts in one week so I was hoping—'

'You have done a lot of talking and texting, Three, but taken no risks whatsoever. One does not get promotion for dumping what no one wants in a place no one visits in a year no one leaps to. Nor for having talented family members. There is no substitute for hard work and skill.

'Which leads me to make the following proposal. After the rotation, we have a vacancy for One. I propose Portia. She is young and has a lot to learn but has proved herself over the years, and this week in particular, to be worthy of The Vicious Circle. Who will second this?'

'I do, Millennia,' says Three, soon to be Four.

'And I,' says Evil Nine.

'Any objections?'

'She shows too much mercy,' says The Grandfather in his high-low voice. 'She messed with me mid-job, in her high-flying car!'

'You shot the wrong girl!' Evil Nine laughs and laughs and I freeze under the table. If they knew I was here, a few feet away from them, what would they do to me? Evil Nine continues. 'You should have left it to me.'

'Your boys failed to fix the 800 metres. Our enemies beat us hollow!'

'Enough of this dissent. Grandfather, I respect your concern. However, I override it. Rise from your seats, everyone. Let each of you from One to Seven move one space clockwise. I will contact Portia. She has the right to refuse but I don't think she will, if she's as wise as I believe her to be.'

There's a scraping of chairs on the oak-panelled floor and I use that opportunity to rub the pins and needles from my legs. Big Ben stretches, sits up and rubs his eyes. His allergies are playing up again. It's an old room and probably hasn't been dusted for weeks. He tips his head back and oh my Chrono, he's going to sneeze! He goes still as a statue for a couple of seconds then relaxes. Thank goodness, I think.

But then it comes: ATISHOO!

It happens during the second scraping of chairs, when everyone takes their new place round the circle. I hold my breath.

'What was that?' Evil Nine.

'What was what?' Millennia.

'I heard a noise. Like a shot.'

'I heard it too.' Three, now Four. 'A shot from the chamber below. Esteemed leader, would you like me to investigate?'

Please don't, I think, my hands clasped together in prayer. If they find us, we're dead!

'I think not,' says Millennia, 'unless Grandfather has been doing target practice.'

Several people laugh and then there's silence.

No one peeps under the table.

No one tells us to come out with our hands above our heads.

We're safe!

For now.

∞

Portia has arrived and taken her place in the vacant seat. Millennia has given a long welcome speech, going into loud-speaker mode three times. It's clear Portia isn't particularly impressed with words. She's a woman of action.

'Esteemed leader, what's my assignment?'

'To recruit new-millennials. I need talented young people and I need the best. So far, I have both failed and triumphed. The Time Squad is dead; it's time for the next step of the grand plan. I am not getting any younger.'

She pauses and I imagine several of The Vicious Circle nodding their heads. No one knows how old Millennia is but according to Ama, she's def over 100!

'What's the grand plan?' says Portia.

'To form a Leapocracy; government by Leapers. Why be led by Annuals when we can foresee? World leaders can only make predictions: Leapers with The Gift can access the future. We KNOW what will happen.'

Meridian shuffles her feet. 'What MIGHT happen, Millennia. You know very well the future is not fixed; it is constantly changing, depending on our present actions.'

'Then we Leapers must act. Seize power and use The Gift to the full!'

'The future is green—'

'THE FUTURE IS GREY. The future is in technology: the internet, smartphones, robots.' I hear the familiar click of a Chronophone being switched on. Millennia's. 'Whoever controls technology, controls minds. And whoever controls minds controls the future.'

Millennia's voice has risen into loudspeaker mode. She sounds properly scary, even worse than when she shouted in my face on last year's trip. I shudder and Big Ben freezes. It's wrong to think Leaplings with The Gift should have more power. Other people have amazing gifts, too. Imagine if Millennia ruled the world! Her dream is our nightmare.

'I get your quest for world domination, esteemed leader,' says Portia. 'But if you want me to recruit the best minds, there are too few Leaplings with The Gift in the world. And if I'm targeting teens, fewer still.'

'Include Annuals.'

'How? Surely it's impossible to prove we have The Gift without revealing it? What about the Oath of Secrecy?'

'BREAK it!'

A hushed silence. No one contradicts Millennia, not even Meridian, but I sense The Vicious Circle are shocked. This is the first time they're hearing this. Big Ben and I do what-big-eyes at each other under the table. Breaking the Oath to gain power or money or fame is the worst thing a Leapling can do. The same for the few Annuals who've sworn it to protect their Leapling relatives, like Ama has for Kwesi. We've always been taught if too many Annuals find out about The Gift, no Leapling will be safe. Bad Annuals will exploit us for money. The Vicious

Circle is proof of what bad Leaplings can do. I hate to think how much worse it would be with bad Annuals, too.

There's a long pause before Portia speaks. 'I'm happy to recruit. But I'll never break the Oath!'

'I admire your spirit,' says Millennia, 'and your honesty. Welcome to The Vicious Circle. Henceforth you will not be referred to as Portia, but as One.'

'Thank you, esteemed leader.'

'And you are permitted to call me Millennia. Your allegiance ceremony will take place next week. But you may commence work immediately. You will find your Chronophone gives you a higher level of access to, for example, the Archives. But not the Treasury or the Anti-Leap.

'I now declare this meeting closed. Four, I wish you to stay behind to brief One about the ceremony. I am sure you will enjoy exercising your vocal chords, now you have been promoted clockwise. I shall be back in 40 minutes to attend to some business.'

∞

Big Ben stops the recording and I smile even though my whole body aches from being under the table so long. We don't have precise details of the latest theft but we know the original sandglass is on the table above us, we know Eight has exited or BEEN exited and we know all about Millennia's grand plan! Four and Portia have left the table and are chatting at the edge of the room. It sounds like they're close to the chamber I leapt to on Monday. It's quite difficult to hear what they're saying, like they're whis-

155

pering. That's odd! Why do they need to whisper unless they're plotting something?

Suddenly they start talking normally again and Four clears his throat.

'Whoever you are, and I believe I can guess, come out from under the table or suffer the consequences.'

∞ Chapter 18:00 ∞

ABOUT TIME

'To gatecrash The Vicious Circle once was an accident, but twice? That's a death wish. Do not assume you can leap out of this. I just activated the Anti-Leap. Our esteemed Millennia is far too lax with security.'

Four is right; we can't leap. We tried from under the table just now and it didn't work. But Millennia's laxness did us a favour: it let us leap here in the first place. I narrow my eyes at him.

'Our friend's in Do-Time for something he didn't do. We're not giving up till he's free!' I say. 'AND one of your members stole a present from a child. Was it Eight?'

'Who delivered the Infinity-Glass to The Vicious Circle? You did. I was totally fooled at the time but Portia here enlightened me. You know too much of our business. It's a pity she didn't run you over outside your school. But knowing your stubbornness, you would still have leapt back to that morning to stop the theft. Unsuccessfully.'

'Not if I'd been killed,' I say. 'But that wasn't meant to be. You can't change what's already happened; you can only change the future and this is how it will be: you in prison, not MC²!'

He winces. 'Delighted to meet you, Elle, Big Ben. The name is Nano, by the way. I prefer it to Four. Four is the name of a nobody.'

'Nano means a billionth,' says Big Ben. 'That's a LOT smaller than Four.'

'Thank you for the clarification.' Nano is still smiling with his mouth but his eyes are hard. Big Ben, 1: Nano, nil! 'Do make yourselves comfortable,' he gestures towards the table, 'you might be here for quite some time.'

'Uncle,' says Portia, 'let's leave. I'll luggage you home. You can give me the briefing another time.'

Big Ben's staring at Portia like he wants to talk cars. I stare at her too and she winks. It's a split-second wink but unmistakable. That means she's still on our side. Now, I'm looking at the chairs around the circle. The original marine sandglass is on the table in front of Millennia's seat. It's odd seeing it here, like it was freshly manufactured in 2021, not 1752. I can't take my eyes off it. The decision is made without speaking. I sit in Millennia's chair and Big Ben sits next to me, in The Grandfather's.

'Delusions of grandeur!' says Nano, his voice trembling. 'But sitting in those chairs will not increase your Gift. You cannot escape. As for the sandglass, it's worth nothing. It has no history. Esteemed Millennia paid a handsome sum for a glimpse of it but it's not even worthy of our Archive.'

He stands next to Big Ben and grabs the sandglass from the

table in his right hand, his eyes slightly glazed. 'This glass is worse than nothing.'

'Uncle, no!' says Portia.

Big Ben stands up abruptly.

Nano launches the Glass across the room and I gasp. This is VERY SERIOUS INDEED! If it breaks, we'll never be able to get it back to Francis, it will never get the carvings and travel through the ages and end up in the Museum of the Past, the Present and the Future to get stolen in the first place. If it breaks, it might rupture the space–time continuum! If it breaks, it will shatter my belief that the past is fixed. It CAN'T break.

The Glass travels high as a shot put then begins its descent.

There's no way I can get to it in time, even with my fast reflexes.

Portia is frozen to the spot so no way is she going to catch it either.

Big Ben flies into the air in what seems like slow motion and stretches out his hands.

He catches it, pulling it close to his body to stop it from breaking.

Portia punches the air. I think she's forgotten she's at The Vicious Circle's headquarters, not a football match, but I'm impressed, too.

'Good save, BB!' I say and inspect the Glass for damage before placing it carefully back onto the table.

Nano frowns. 'You can keep but you can't leap. I have not been sufficiently entertained. So, here's a Vicious Circle challenge: you have half an hour to escape from this chamber. If you fail—'

'Uncle, I don't think—' says Portia.

'—you will face the wrath of Millennia.'

A fate worse than death!

'You understand,' he continues, 'it won't be EXACTLY 30 minutes. You cannot trust the ancient timekeepers.'

Nano upturns the marine sandglass and the black sand begins to flow . . .

∞

We send a megatext to The Infinites:

URGENT VC stole sandglass. Trapped at VC. Strong Anti-Leap. MM back 30 mins. HELP!

GMT leaps all over the timeline so maybe she's overcome Anti-Leap before and can tell us what to do.

Kwesi's clever and used to be a bit wild so he might think outside the box and come up with a plan.

MC^2 is likely to be in his cell and his phone will be buzzing in a locker in a different part of the building. That gives me an idea.

'What about Bonzo?' I say, remembering the young, red-headed prison warden.

I copy the text and send it to 3442. If Bonzo gets it, at least he can tell MC^2, who's an expert on mind over matter.

Big Ben and I hold hands and squeeze our eyes tight shut to leap again but nothing happens. We've tried so many times, we're exhausted. Big Ben's attempted to hack into the system on his Chronophone. We've searched under the table for activation switches. Now we're walking round the edge of the room, pushing the hidden panels in case there's a control room behind one of the doors. Nothing has worked. Nano smiles his oily smile.

Minutes feel like hours.

If I look at the sandglass, I'm hypnotised by the flow of the sand.

If I look at my watch, time's like a heartbeat pumping the seconds.

If I look at my Chronophone, time expands into all possible time and space and the continuum overwhelms me.

Twenty minutes have gone by: less than ten minutes left. I take deep breaths. I refuse to let The Vicious Circle beat me. We have to escape; we have to get this sandglass back to Francis; we have to find evidence to free MC². I look across at Portia. She winked at us; surely she's going to help?

Nano has been briefing her about the allegiance ceremony, both of them tapping into their Chronophones, when a ring tone starts coming from Nano's. He answers it.

'Yes . . . No, we're almost done . . . Does it have to be now, Anno? I'll only be a few more . . . Very well, coming!' He turns to us. 'I have to take my leave. How disappointing to miss the grand finale!' He taps rapidly into his phone.

'I'll transport you, Uncle,' says Portia.

She holds both of Nano's hands, tilts her head to the right and concentrates. 'Back in a SECOND.'

Big Ben and I are taken by surprise at her emphasis and in the blink of an eye, Portia's back.

'Bother!' she says. 'I texted Mum to get her to text Uncle

pretending she had an emergency. It worked, no questions asked. Mum trusts me more than anyone else. But you're still here. I wanted you to leap free the second Uncle deactivated the Anti-Leap but had no way of telling you without him knowing.' She sighs. 'But I leapt back to check. Now I'm stuck here too. I can't control security; sand's almost run out; then Millennia will be back.'

I check my phone. We only have four minutes left, probably less. I look at Big Ben.

'What do we do?'

'We leap when Millennia appears. Anti-Leap will be off. She can't leap to a nanosecond, she's too old.'

Big Ben's right. I remember how haggard she looked after leaping on summer solstice. But Portia's frowning.

'A bit risky. What if we mistime it? I could text Mum again, she might be able to help, she knows I'm helping you. We need a plan—'

A gush of air, the outline of a boy and my heart is pounding in my chest. A split second later, MC^2 appears on top of the table.

'Sorry, Leaps,' he says, 'took time to beat the Anti-Leap!'

'You leapt out of Do-Time! That's a criminal offence. They'll arrest you and put you back in prison for longer!' I say, but I smile, pleased to see him.

'No need, I'm free! I leapt from my yard. Some anonymous Leap bailed me. I'm free to leap where an' when I like. Till the trial anyways. Got your text on my Chronophone. They don't call me MC^2 for nothing, I bin in training. Prison focuses body an' mind; needed both to break in here! Now we can Chrono an' defeat the Anti-Leap.'

'About time!' says Portia.

'What do you mean?' I say.

'I've been waiting all my life to meet MC^2 and here he is! I'm such a fan, you wouldn't imagine.'

MC^2 shrugs but I can see he's flattered. Then he sees the sandglass on the table and shakes his head.

'This the Glass? Who'd thieve that?'

'That's what I thought,' says Portia. 'But I guess it's useful on a ship. And Millennia would prefer it plain. Infinity symbols remind her of Infinity, bring her out in a cold sweat; but she loves anything from the 18th century.'

'More importantly, it's the original, special to Francis,' I say.

'Little man deserves better!' MC^2 does his thinking frown. 'Elle, your Grandma working late again?'

I nod. Grandma's been doing far too many shifts this week. When she gets home, she always looks exhausted, like she's leapt a century.

'Right. That's our first stop.'

Big Ben says, 'Don't we leap back to 1752?'

and I say, 'What about Francis?'

at exactly the same time.

'We gotta leap, Leaps! The Mush-Rooms. Now! You want Millennia to join us?'

'Can I leap with you?' says Portia. 'It'll seem suspicious if Millennia gets back and finds me here without Uncle.'

'She's right,' I say. 'Portia's helped us. We need to help her.

163

And we need to beat the Anti-Leap – the more of us, the better!'

The four of us form a Chrono, place the sandglass in the middle and concentrate. It's hard, like leaping through half-set concrete and I feel nauseous the whole time because I haven't got any leap bands.

But we do it.

We land in the middle of my kitchen, narrowly missing the cooker. Portia gives us a big smile.

'That was amazing, thanks guys.' She pauses. 'I'd better go, but keep up the great work!' She disappears into thin air.

I wouldn't describe it as amazing. Torture, more like. While I'm retching, MC^2 is tapping into his Chronophone. He laughs and high-fives the air!

'Kwesi's joining us. He's bringing some tools an' spit. Elle, Big Ben, take one last look at the sandglass before it gets a makeover, Infinite style.'

∞ Chapter 19:00 ∞

MAKING HISTORY

It takes them all evening to carve the infinity symbols into the sandglass. They take it in turns. MC^2 does a LOT of body blinking and the Glass looks suspiciously different each time he does, like he leapt forward or back in time to buy an extra hour or two then leapt back a split second later, his eyes wide with innocence. Kwesi doesn't cheat though. He does less carving and more trying on and sorting black gloves of all sizes like the ones Tommie Smith and John Carlos wore to do their Black Power salute at the 1968 Olympics.

'Why are you doing that?' I say and Kwesi twists his hands.

'Further customisation,' says MC^2, translating. 'Wait till we give it to Francis an' you'll see.'

I hear someone come through the front door downstairs and frown. Grandma shouldn't be back yet. I open the flat door to check. If Grandma's back, she'll probably be OK about me having friends round. She's always pleased to see my friends. But I always find it hard being around Grandma AND my friends at the same time. I prefer to meet them separately because we discuss different things. It's hard having two conversations at the same time. I poke my head out of the door. Oh no! It's the landlord coming up the stairs.

'Hello, Elle,' he says, 'Is your Grandma at home?'

'No,' I say.

'Do you know when she'll be back because,' he smiles with his mouth but not his eyes, 'she owes me two months' rent.'

'I don't know,' I say, which is true. 'She's doing an extra cleaning job.'

'I'm so pleased to hear that, Elle. Because then she'll have the rent money.'

'Yes,' I say, hoping he'll go away but he doesn't.

'Are you sure she's not in? I heard voices.'

'I'm with my friends.'

The same time I say that, MC^2 calls out from the kitchen.

'Elle. Everything OK?'

'Sorry to disturb you, Elle,' says the landlord. 'Give this to your Grandma.'

He hands me a typed letter on a crumpled piece of paper. I look at the heading: EVICTION NOTICE. I shut the door, feeling sick. I didn't know we owed TWO months' rent. I knew Grandma was cross when the rent increased but I didn't realise she hadn't been paying it. How can she spend so many hours working yet we still don't have enough money for rent? I scan the letter. It looks like we have four weeks to pay before we have to leave the flat.

I turn back to my friends. Big Ben's eating a squashed cheese sandwich from his bag; MC² is focusing on the Glass and Kwesi's signing something to him. I don't want to think about money problems; I want to think about us Leaplings making history in weird and wonderful ways because we have The Gift of time-travel. Kwesi and MC² are customising the marine sandglass NOW, in 2021, so it becomes the Infinity-Glass and we WILL manage to deliver it back to Francis in 1752 where it belongs because how else could it exist and age through history for over 250 years and end up as the ancient, worn artefact that was stolen from the Museum of the Past, the Present and the Future?

The ANCIENT version needs to be discovered and taken back to the museum where it belongs. But first things first. This glass is freshly carved; it looks amazing with its swirly ∞ symbols. MC² turns to Kwesi.

'You gonna accompany us to brighten up little man Francis or leap back to '49 an' spray graffiti?'

It's not really a question. This evening, Kwesi's been back to his old self. Now MC² is out on bail, and we're one step closer to proving his innocence, wherever MC² is going, Kwesi's going too.

∞

We decide to leap to early evening of the same day we left. That gives Mistress Anna and Francis a bit of time to calm down and make it seem more plausible we've had time to get the Glass back AND customise it. Francis knows we're Leaplings but we have to assume Mistress Anna doesn't. I don't completely trust her. Maybe she stole the Glass and made up the story about

Anon. Maybe she's a Leapling in disguise, another one of Nano's evil sisters!

The stench hits me again as we land. I'll never get used to it. I fumble in my bag for a sweet. Old Meg's sitting in the alley, huddled up in a dirty brown shawl. I think she's asleep but when I start to move away, she clutches my skirt.

'Mark my words. Your gentlewoman friend is an odd 'n!'

'She's autistic, not odd,' I say. But Old Meg wouldn't understand autism. It wasn't recognised in 1752.

'Yesterday you witnessed she gave me shillings. This morning, not even a how do you do, Old Meg? And it's not the first time, neither.'

'Was she in a hurry?'

'Hurry is not the word. A hurly-burly. Her stick barely touched the ground and I wager if I had greeted her, she would have struck me with it! Warning: she is not to be trusted!'

'Thank you for telling us. My name's Elle. Please tell us if you remember anything else. We don't have money, but would you like a sweet?'

'Thank you, kind miss. God reward you!'

I like Old Meg. I hope she's telling the truth and has just given us another clue.

∞

When we get to the house, Francis opens the door. Mistress Anna has gone upstairs to lie down in her room and GMT's sitting exactly where she was before.

'Hi guys,' she says, 'you sure took your time.'

'Lots has happened,' I say. 'We found the hourglass and heard about Millennia's grand plan and got captured but MC^2 helped us escape and the rest is a secret soon to be revealed!'

Francis looks happy to see me and Big Ben but when he sees Kwesi and MC^2 appear behind us, he leaps out of his seat, runs over and hugs them like he's a small child. He hasn't even noticed the sandglass. It's like he's forgotten all about the theft.

'You came back!' he says. 'Now I have my big brothers, everything is perfect.'

'We got you a present,' says MC^2. 'Well, we customised it so you remember us. Not just me an' Kwesi but Elle an' Big Ben an' GMT. We all swore allegiance last year.'

He means we did The Infinite ceremony but that's top secret. Only The Infinites and Infinity know we exist. MC^2 carefully puts the decorated sandglass on the table and Francis's eyes go bigger than Jupiter.

'You rescued it from the thief. And engraved it! How did you make these carvings so quickly? Is it magic?'

'Not exactly,' MC^2 sits on one of the chairs and looks left and right like he's making sure no one else is in the room.

'How did you do it, then?'

'You know we can trek through time, bro? The thief did too so we hunted down your glass in 2021 and Kwesi an' me spent some hours working on it before we came back to now.'

'So you really ARE from the future?'

'Yeah! Your present is our past. But Leaps forget that spit most o' the time. We can't break history but we CAN make it.

Anyways, we got you somethin' extra as an honorary Leap. Give him the glove, Kwesi.'

Kwesi dips into his pocket and produces one of his black gloves. Francis puts it on his right hand. Then Kwesi guides Francis's hand flat over the top of the Glass and something amazing happens.

Gradually, grain by grain, the sand starts flowing upwards!

Kwesi's futuristic gloves are acting like a powerful magnet, making the sand do the opposite to normal. Now the Infinity-Glass is even more special: like my name, Elle, that reads the same both ways; like Leaplings leaping to the past or the future. Francis shrieks with excitement and MC^2 high-fives his left hand. Kwesi does the same. I've never seen a ten-year-old boy look so happy. After a minute or two of being mesmerised, Francis looks up at us.

'I am overwhelmed with your kindness and talent. How can I repay you?'

'You don't need to,' I say. 'We don't want money!'

'Very well,' says Francis, 'since I value your company above everything.'

He clears his throat like he's a grown-up about to make a speech.

'You must ALL come to my gathering here on September the 2nd.' He pauses. 'This sandglass will be the centrepiece. When the Master bestowed the gift upon me this morning, he said it would remind me of the sea and the forthcoming leap. But now it will additionally remind me that I have friends who can travel backwards and forwards in time.

'This is the best present in HISTORY!'

∞ Chapter 20:00 ∞

THE 2ND OF SEPTEMBER
1752

I t's the night of the 11-day leap!
We leapt from Friday the 25th of June after school when it was scorching hot but Wednesday the 2nd of September 1752 is much much cooler. As soon as we land in the alley, church bells strike 8 o'clock and Old Meg has something to say to us.

''Tis the busiest night ever for apparitions. Rich pickings for pickpockets. It must be due to the strange stealing of time.'

I give her a leap sweet and she gives me a toothless smile.

Francis answers the door at Gough Square. I can tell he's excited because he's speaking even more quickly than usual.

'Mistress Anna is busy in the kitchen. And I must light the candles. And after this gathering, we will set forth for the Carnival of the Calendar! We're having patties. Master will receive you in the drawing-room shortly. So much to do!'

He climbs the first flight of stairs to the candle cupboard and I'm reminded that's where he hid the sandglass. The smell of pastry wafts up the stairs and makes my mouth water. Francis continues talking as he comes back down.

'I hope you have brought poems about Time. MC² told me he excels at rhyming and Anon informs me that you, Elle, have won a poetry competition!'

'Anon's here?'

'She is. Poetry is her passion. And in very good spirits tonight. She has not assaulted me with questions about timepieces.'

When Francis is ready, we turn right at the top of the stairs to see they have opened the panel completely so the room's open plan and much larger than on our first visit. The light is already fading and the lit candles make shadows dance on the ceiling. It's very atmospheric and excitement tingles in my stomach. The chairs are arranged in a semi-circle, Mr Johnson and Anno sitting at the far side. For a split second, I see an image of the sinister full circle headed by Millennia but I push the thought out of my mind. We still need to prove MC²'s innocence before the trial AND find the ancient Infinity-Glass but tonight's a night off. I'm here to enjoy myself.

The new Infinity-Glass has been placed on a small table in the middle of the room, like it's the guest of honour.

Francis announces us as if he's a grown-up in a play.

'I present Elle Bíbi Imbelé Ifíè; Benedykt Novak; Kwesi Atta Asante; GMT and MC².'

We all bow and curtsy. Mr Johnson has dressed for the

occasion in a purple jacket with fraying sleeves. He tilts his head to the right when he hears the name MC^2, reminding me of something but I can't think what. Big Ben's staring intently at Mr Johnson and frowning. Then our host smiles and says in his booming voice:

'A most peculiar but pleasing name, young gentleman. You may inform me of its mathematical meaning later. I am always seeking new terminology.

'Welcome, thief-catchers and wood-engravers, to our literary salon. Please be seated. Tonight, there will be potion, patties and poetry. The potion is tea, the patties are subject to the local baker's culinary skill and the poetry is in honour of Time.'

'And do not forget to honour this exquisite sandglass,' says Anon, 'nor the infinity biscuits I have especially baked and iced.'

She looks at me intently through her glasses when she says iced. She knows I mostly eat white food and has made the effort so I have something to eat, which is kind. But how do I know I can trust Anon after she almost definitely stole the sandglass the day Francis received it? How did she know the infinity symbols would already be on it unless she'd visited again and been snooping? I don't know whether to say thank you or not. If I say thank you it will be polite but I won't totally mean it; if I say nothing it will be rude and I don't want to be rude. But in the space when I COULD speak, something happens.

Mistress Anna reaches the top of the stairs with a large tray, peers into the room and shrieks. The tray full of teapot, teacups, milk and sugar falls to the ground with a loud crash! You wouldn't believe the mess; it looks like a bomb has landed.

Anon rises from her chair with her stick. 'Oh, Mistress Anna. Let me assist you in—'

'NO!' shouts Mistress Anna. 'Stay away from me, spirit!'

GMT is also on her feet ready to help but Mr Johnson has crossed the room and is supporting his housekeeper, who looks ready to faint.

'I require your assistance,' he says to GMT. 'For, contrary to your male attire, I sense you are of the female sex. Since it would be improper for me to enter the room of a gentlewoman, please enable Mistress Anna to reach her room comfortably. It is clear she needs both repose and smelling salts. Francis, fetch the latter. And a stout broom!'

I feel sorry for Mistress Anna because she's a poet, not only a housekeeper, but now she won't have the chance to read at the salon. AND I know why she fainted. We all know except Mr Johnson. But Anon's pretending to be in shock.

'Upon my word, I have never seen Mistress Anna so disordered. Whatever can have ailed her?'

'Musta bin somethin' she saw,' says MC^2.

There's an awkward silence while Francis collects the broom and starts sweeping rather ineffectively, like he's never handled a broom in his life. GMT is obviously staying with Mistress Anna in her room, opposite. I'm glad she's here to help like she did before. If it was me helping, I wouldn't know what to do or say. If it had been me who felt shaky, I'd just want to be left alone. Mr Johnson doesn't seem to notice how tense we all are.

'Well,' he says, 'it is fortunate I have such a liking for tea that the entire house is composed of tea cups. I have another set in this very room which Francis will set up once he has finished sweeping.'

'Kind sir, though I am a guest, since Mistress Anna is indisposed I am more than willing to remake the tea but I shall need some young assistants. Elle and Big Ben, would you oblige?'

It would be very difficult to say no so we both follow Anon down two flights of stairs to the basement kitchen. It's dark and gloomy with only one tiny window. Anon attends to the kettle which is hung over the fire and instructs us to find plates for the patties being kept warm beside it. It takes us a while to find them: the cupboards are chaos. Food seems to be mixed with the crockery. I feel a bit dizzy from trying to concentrate in this new space. Then I realise why it's worse: I'm hungry. My senses are heightened.

Big Ben finds some plain white plates covered in dust but they'll be OK after a wipe. I remove the off-white cloth covering the food and frown. They don't look like Jamaican patties I've seen before. They look like pies someone trod on but they smell delicious, savoury and spicy. Maybe Mr Johnson ordered them especially for Francis because he's originally from Jamaica. That would be a nice touch. I might even try one myself wearing my futuristic glasses. I rarely eat meat these days but this is a VERY SPECIAL OCCASION.

Anon has been busy finding milk and sugar for the tea but now she turns to us.

'I must say, you are both uncommonly quiet this evening. What is it?'

'We're tired,' I say. 'It's been a busy week.'

That's not untrue; it HAS been a busy week.

'Will you both be attending Anno's private view tomorrow afternoon?'

'Yes.'

'Let me extend the invitation to your older friends. I hope you have sufficient time to rest before then. However, I suspect you will be out at the Carnival tonight, like all Leaplings who enjoy this leap more than Annuals do.'

'Maybe.'

Out of the corner of my eye I see a tall, hooded shadow pass the window. I blink and it's gone. It reminds me of something but I can't think what. The Vicious Circle? They wear hooded gowns. But this person was taller than Millennia and Nano. I look at Big Ben. He obviously didn't see the figure. Too busy thinking about the food! I can't tell him about it right now with Anon here. I shudder and my heart starts racing. The evening's spoilt already. But at least it's taught me something important: you can't have a night off when you're on a mission. You need to be on high alert!

∞

Back upstairs, MC² is finishing a rap:

> '. . . the split
> second peeps leapt while they slept on the
> 2nd of Sept.'

Kwesi and Francis high-five MC² and each other while Mr Johnson applauds.

'I enjoyed your song very much, young gentleman, though I did not understand a single syllable due to its verbal velocity. What style is it?'

'Freestyle rap, Your Honour,' says MC².

I smile because that's how you address a judge in court. Mr Johnson's wearing a wig like a judge so that must have made MC² say that. Then I stop smiling because I remember that he'll be charged in court soon unless we come up with evidence.

We put the patties and kettle on the table next to the fresh tea set and the battered oak box that Mr Johnson calls a tea caddy. Anon makes the tea and everyone helps themselves. I put on my colour-coolers and adjust the settings till the patties are a very pale grey. Not ideal but I'm too hungry to fiddle for too long. I take a big bite and enjoy the mixture of minced beef, hot spices and thick pastry.

'And next,' says Mr Johnson, 'I introduce Elle who has, I understand, produced a poem in honour of the sandglass.'

I wish I hadn't started the patty now. My stomach does somersaults as I stand up to read:

177

Is infinity ingrained in 11 missing days?
Formed in the leap year 1752
this maritime sandglass
sparkling black sand
flows the same as,
letter by letter,
my name
E
L
L
E
my name,
letter by letter,
flows the same as
sparkling black sand.
This maritime sandglass
formed in the leap year 1752
is infinity ingrained in 11 missing days.

Mr Johnson is extremely excited. His whole seated body is moving, face, hands and feet as he listens. I find it distracting though I know he can't help it. When I finish, he claps his hands.

'Young madam, your poem was awful!'

I can't believe he just said that. If my poem was so bad, why's he applauding it? But Anon quickly explains.

'Mr Johnson finds your poem awe-inspiring.'

Then I realise awful is one of those funny words that change meaning over time, like when Ama says wreckage. Mr Johnson is still applauding.

'You have invented an entirely new form, a veritable palindrome that, like your name, reads the same backwards as forwards.'

'I didn't invent it,' I say.

'No matter. You have stimulated my intellect.' He turns to Big Ben, 'Now, young gentleman, I understand that you prefer mathematics to linguistics,' he pauses, 'but we accommodate all languages in this house, except French.'

'Mr Johnson, you are being mischievous,' says Anon.

'Madam, I am, for were you to hear my French, you would vacate the room! Big Ben, you are a man of numbers and I am a man of letters. Let us shake hands in mutual respect.'

I'm glad Mr Johnson acknowledged Big Ben, even though he doesn't have a poem. Mr Johnson smiles.

'Kwesi, let me call upon you.'

Just before Kwesi begins, GMT appears from Mistress Anna's room. She gives the thumbs up so we know the housekeeper's OK and takes a seat beside Anon.

Kwesi signs an original poem about the Infinity-Glass: '∞ 8'. He's the most inventive of all because he uses his own sign language that only he and MC^2 fully understand. It's like a dance. He makes florid movements and clicks his fingers. Mr Johnson is very impressed. Then he clears his throat so we know he is going to make an important announcement.

'Thank you, one and all. This evening was for young Frank,

who writes a pretty signature, is an excellent listener but has not yet taken to formal literature,' Mr Johnson looks at MC^2 to see if he's appreciated the wordplay. MC^2 high-fives him and he continues.

'Frank, I trust hearing your friends has inspired you for the future. And young friends, I trust you will keep Frank safe on your nightly excursion while Anon and I discuss the intricacies of the heroic couplet. Before you take your leave, hark the bells of St Bride's! St Martin's follows. Fellow poets, it is the 11th hour. Let us toast the Leap-Glass before they embezzle our 11 days!'

'To the Leap-Glass!' we say, and our clinking of teacups is accompanied by a chorus of bells of all shapes of sound.

'St Paul's, and finally St Dunstan-in-the-West!' says Mr Johnson.

We listen to the bells till they fade into silence. For a split second there is no sound at all and then we hear it: the 11 chimes of St Dunstan-in-the-West.

One hour to go before the great leap!

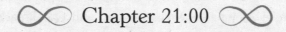 Chapter 21:00

CARNIVAL OF THE CALENDAR

The festival's taking place in fields north of the city but we hear its classical music before we see it. There's a long, snaking queue outside which gives me time to adjust to the sights and sounds. Teens in long green velvet robes are handing out ear-defenders and colour-coolers like mine. I take the ear-defenders just in case. GMT greets one of them, a young woman with long brown hair down to her waist and nothing on her feet. She must be freezing! The air's cool and damp and smells of woodsmoke.

'Never knew you guys were coming, Zilla.'

'We neither, it was last minute. Come see us in the back field. The Daisy-Chain.'

Francis is so excited he looks like he's going to explode. He hasn't stopped talking since we left the house.

'. . . and a Masquerade and Illuminations never heretofore seen and many more Spectacles . . .' he reads off a crumpled leaflet.

181

We reach the front of the queue and look up.

CARNIVAL OF THE CALENDAR says a banner in huge swirly letters like a signature.

There are large, stripy, pointy tents and small open stages. It's a riot of colour and sound and smell. The man to the left of the entrance has long brown greasy hair and a pockmarked face. His clothes are made of coarse cloth. The woman on the right is tall, with fading brown hair like her full-length dress. She looks familiar. Francis shows his advance ticket and the man raises his eyebrows.

'Look, our Meg!' he says. 'We got an Annual!'

I look at the woman called Meg and she winks at me. It's Old Meg looking 20 years younger! It must have been powder in her hair to make it look white. Maybe if she looks VERY old, people feel extra sorry for her and she makes more money from begging or maybe it's 18th-century fashion to make yourself look older. She still looks old and wrinkled but much more alive. I call her New Meg in my head.

'Fear not, Tom,' she says, 'he's in good company.'

Francis is too excited to take this in. He pays a shilling each for all of us, New Meg clips day-glo lanyards onto our wrists and waves us in. But just as I'm passing, she grabs my arm and speaks so softly, even I strain to hear her.

'Take heed, Elle. I heard your name in the alley this night. There's trouble afoot.'

'Thanks,' I say.

I'm thankful to get the warning but not for what it might mean. I'd forgotten about the hooded shadow I saw earlier; now

182

I'm going to spend the whole evening on edge. I don't think anyone else heard but Kwesi looks at me, checking to see if I'm OK. I swallow the nerves building up in my stomach. If I tell my friends, I'll feel safer, but I don't want to ruin their night. They'd spend the whole evening being worried about me.

People are wandering around, standing in groups or queuing at brightly painted wooden food stalls. The smell of baked potatoes and toffee apples fills the air. There's a whole pig roasting on a spit and a yellow stall selling hot punch. Beside it, a booth with people sitting outside is called Veggie Tables. Of course, there's food from all over the timeline. Food stalls line the entire edge of the field.

There are white people, black people, mixed-race people, Indian, Chinese, South American people; women in hooped skirts; mini-skirts, multi-coloured wrappers and bell-bottomed jeans like GMT's 1960s chic; shimmering all-in-one shellsuits; men in tall top hats, men with greased-back hair in dinner jackets; men in robes; men in metal helmets; teenagers with spiky, luminescent dinosaur hairstyles and tartan trousers; teens in hoodies; toddlers in flashing traffic-light trainers; babies in slings; babies in bonnets; babies in backpacks.

I look at Francis and Francis looks at me. His eyes are too big for his head!

'Are they all Leaplings? Do you know them? My ticket entitles me to free food and drink but I can furnish you with more shillings if you desire it.'

'Glad we ain't still queuing,' says MC². 'Didn't wanna miss The Squared on stage.'

Kwesi raises his eyebrows high and MC² shrugs.

'I gigged this fest before, bro.'

'You should have told us,' I say. 'What if you bump into yourself?'

'Lotsa Leaps double up tonight. It's a one-off.'

'Aren't they all breaking the Oath coming in crowds? What about Annuals seeing? Won't they call the police?'

'Anyone up this late and in this field is far out, man,' says GMT.

'Or out for a profit,' says MC². 'London's a square mile and we're outside it. They ain't got no real police force yet. The 18th-century Leaps run stuff. They bin advertising for weeks in the backstreets. Heard of the frost fairs? This is the field fest!'

I HAVE heard of frost fairs even before Francis mentioned them beside the Thames. People partied on the River Thames when it froze solid in the winter and once they even had an ELEPHANT on ice! They sound amazing.

'I want to go to a frost fair!' says Francis. 'Can you take me?'

'Maybe, bro. Next one's in '67 but it ain't worth a Chrono. Best one's the finale in 1814. I could luggage you but it's a heap of a leap.' GMT gives him a nudge. 'Maybe not.'

'Come on guys, let's go see some action,' says GMT, seeing Francis's disappointment. 'Who wants to hang out at the Daisy-Chain?'

∞

The Daisy-Chain's a dome tent the size of Mr Johnson's drawing-room, with swirly patterns all over it. It's a bunch of hippies playing music from 1968 on an audio cassette player which people used in the olden days. They either have very long, uncombed straggly hair parted in the middle or afros in crazy colours like purple or green. 1968's my favourite year so I'm in my element. They're playing this amazing song called 'For Once In My Life' but Kwesi and MC² make the same face Grandma makes when the pepper soup isn't spicy enough.

'I'm not in the vibe but Leaps can hang if they like.'

'Sure will,' says GMT. 'Catch you by the green stage at midnight.'

'Midnight's too late. You don't wanna miss countdown. Five to.'

'OK, guys. You gonna take Francis?'

'No probs. What about you, big bro?'

Big Ben smiles. 'I like it here.'

'Laters, then,' says MC² and off they go.

I love spending time in the Daisy-Chain. I get to relax and a free 1968 audio cassette from Zilla who promises to get me a machine to play it on when I get home, via GMT. That's a kind thing to do. GMT gets to chat with her friends. Big Ben seems to like Zilla, who has a habit of flicking her extremely long hair over her shoulder. Big Ben seems mesmerised by the action but suddenly turns to me looking excited.

'Mr Johnson leans his head like the thief in the video.'

'Well spotted, BB. But I don't think he's the thief. He's too large!'

We both smile. It's just as well we're having downtime now: it prepares us for what happens next.

∞

'10, 9, 8, 7, 6, 5, 4, 3, 2, 1,' chant the crowd. 'ZERO!'

Wednesday the 2nd of September becomes Thursday the 14th!

There are loud bangs like gunshots and 11 missiles shoot into the sky, exploding into bright white light and so much smoke you could see it on the south coast! Then they change colour to red and green. Fireworks but not as I know them. At the same time, they ramp up the classical music. I fumble in my bag for the ear defenders. I LOVE the visuals but have never been great with loud, sudden noises. The music's uplifting though; it holds onto your heart and makes it thump with joy.

With each set of explosions, the displays become more spectacular. Then I realise they're fireworks through the ages. The final ones scrawl a message in the sky in sparkly silver writing: 1752. The year itself explodes and eleven dates fall through the sky in old-fashioned, spiky handwriting, September the 3rd to September the 13th. Dates that will never exist!

The crowd cheers so loud, I'm thankful for my ear defenders. Then I hear a low, familiar whirring noise that increases in intensity. It can't be. It IS! A flying car display, 11 bright-green futuristic mean machines glowing in the night sky. They duck and dive in perfect formation and I have to look away, remembering what it felt like flying in Portia's Lamborghini. Just watching makes me want to throw up. But I wonder if Season's

186

Ferrari Forever is up there? It would be great to catch up with her again. Big Ben's whooping and Francis is jumping for joy. It's the best thing he's EVER seen.

∞

MC^2 guides us to the far side of the field to an open stage that looks like wooden crates squashed together. A dense crowd has gathered but we manage to weave our way in. I take deep breaths to keep calm. I don't mind standing in crowds but always feel panicked moving through them. A man in a top hat is blocking my view. When I move to see better, I accidentally disturb him and he turns round to glare at me. I jump. He looks like an older version of The Grandfather! But he turns back round again so he can't be. I relax but can't help checking the crowd for purple hoodies. I'm still wondering about the hooded figure I saw earlier. And New Meg's warning.

Einstein is the stage host. He's a friend of MC^2, a muscular black teen wearing a lime-green tracksuit and bright white trainers.

'Next up,' he says, in a deep, breathless voice, 'the best act you NEVER saw! Give it up for M C SQUARED.'

I gasp when I see who comes onto the stage. This is MC^2 but not the one we know; it's a younger version with shorter funky dreads, blinking so much with nerves we can barely see his eyes. He walks to the centre of the stage, disappears and reappears on the spot. That's his speciality. The crowd cheers. Next, he does it across the stage and back again. The cheering gets louder.

Then, he disappears for several seconds and reappears in the audience and the crowd start shouting and swearing with over-excitement. My ear defenders aren't sophisticated enough to block out the cursing. I turn to the older MC^2 beside me.

'What happens next? Do you do any—?'

'Awesome!' says a familiar voice behind me.

I freeze, not because it's someone bad but at the unexpected surprise. Without thinking, everyone closes in around Francis to protect him. But it's Portia. Of course she'd be here; music's her thing. She's dressed in a silver sequinned tracksuit, her peacock hair a bit less spiky than usual.

'How long have you been here?' I say.

'Not long enough. Elle, I've come to warn you. Meridian, The Grandfather and Millennia had a Meeting of the Elders. Something's going to happen but I don't know what.'

Big Ben shakes his head. 'Not logical. How do you know if you weren't there? And how did you know we're here?'

'I can't explain! Just that Elle has to leap back to 2021 and . . .' her voice quivers '. . . stop celebrating non-events in leap years!'

What she just said reminds me of something. I have a sense of déjà vu. I wish I knew what it was. The crowd cheer MC^2 for his freestyle rap.

'It's not a non-event, it's the 11-day leap,' says Big Ben

and I say, 'Can't I stay to the end of the Carnival?'

at exactly the same time.

Portia shakes her head. 'This isn't the time for debate. You can't take on the bad guys alone.' She glances to her right. 'Look!

You can't hide under tables forever; you need an inside ally. I'm working for them but I'm on YOUR side.'

I frown. 'Like a double agent?'

'Yes. And I KNOW you're in danger. Trust me.'

I trust her. She's the opposite of a backfriend. But she could be mistaken about me being in danger tonight.

'Prove it,' says Big Ben.

'On our right are two hooded figures. I saw them prowling outside Mr Johnson's house earlier. They arrived here just after you.'

My heart sinks. That fits with the figure I saw through the kitchen window. Without moving my head, I look to my right and she's right. Two hooded figures at the edge of the crowd are staring straight at us.

'What's happening?'

'I don't know but it doesn't look good. Leap with me, Elle. The others can look after your young friend.'

'I'm coming too!' says Big Ben.

'OK. But only you. We need to get out of the crowd to form a Chrono. Leave now, to our left!'

No time to say goodbye to anyone. We weave our way through brightly dressed revellers until we're at the edge of the crowd. I try not to see if the hooded figures have moved. We hold hands and concentrate. Portia directs.

'Destination, the Music, Maths and Music entrance; date, Friday 25 June.'

'What ti—'

The word freezes in my throat and my whole body suddenly

feels cold. I'm dwarfed by a tall, hooded shadow on my right-hand side, feel a heavy hand on my shoulder as an identical shadow towers over my left.

'Elle Bíbi Imbelé Ifíè,' says a deep, robotic voice. 'We of the Bissextile Investigation Division arrest you for the theft of the Infinity-Glass on Monday the 21st of June 2021 at 9:21.22. Anything you say may be taken as evidence against you . . .'

∞ Chapter 22:00 ∞

THIEF-TAKING

I'm sitting at a table in a square white room with no windows. There's a glass of water in front of me, untouched. Opposite me is the interrogator, a mixed-race woman wearing a white shirt and dark-brown trousers. Her hair's in long braids, parted down the middle. It's her job to ask me questions.

'Don't worry, Elle,' she says. 'We haven't told your Grandma. Mrs C Eckler is on her way.'

I nod. I was worried if they told Grandma I'd been arrested she'd have a heart attack. Luckily, they brought me back to 6 p.m. on Friday 25th of June, so Grandma's still at her cleaning job.

'Are you hungry? I could get you a sandwich or some soup.'

I shake my head.

This is my chance to talk, to tell my side of the story, but I'm tongue-tied. The shock of being arrested, being luggaged from 1752 back to 2021, is too much. Everything is too much.

Didn't Portia say something about kids who know too much? Didn't she say, 'Stop celebrating non-events in leap years'?

I know too much.

And now, everything I know makes sense.

I know who stole the Glass from Mr Johnson's house; I know who stole it from the museum; and I know where it is now!

'Elle, in your own time, tell us what happened at the museum on Monday the 21st of June.'

There's a knock on the door and a male officer appears followed by Mrs C Eckler wearing a 1950s dress with purple flowers on it. Her ginger hair is slipping out of its bun and she looks upset but her voice is calm.

'Elle,' she says, 'I know you're innocent.'

But how can she know? She's not me. She doesn't live in my skin.

Mrs C Eckler might not know what it feels like to BE me but she knows me well. She knows that in the past few months, when I haven't been able to speak, I have been able to write.

The only way to record my story is for me to type it. It's going to be difficult; when your friends are also your enemies, it's a no-win situation. But I have to tell the truth. I can't let them know all the stuff about The Vicious Circle because they could give me two extra charges for breaking and entering but the first time was by mistake and the second was to get the hourglass back to Francis. Anyway, I don't have enough evidence against them. Not yet. But I can tell the police enough to solve both thefts of the Glass, the 1752 and the 2021. Now I know the truth: there were two thefts; there were also two thieves!

∞

The interrogator finishes reading my statement and raises her eyebrows.

'Thank you, Elle,' she says. 'You're a very brave girl.'

She taps into her phone and a minute later, there's another knock on the door. Two female officers this time. The taller one smiles at me.

'Elle. We are pleased to say that your typed statement matches that of an independent witness. There has been a confession. You are free to go!'

It takes a few moments for me to process what's just happened.

Someone's confessed.

Grandma won't have a heart attack.

Mrs C Eckler can drive me home in her bright red Audi Ur-Quattro.

I raise the glass of water to my lips and drink. It's ice-cold, exactly what I need.

'Before you go, Elle, we need to discuss your role at the private view tomorrow afternoon at the museum. We need you to remain on the itinerary as planned, to read your poem. However we would like you to help us secure essential evidence instead. But only if you feel comfortable.'

'What do I have to do?' My voice has come back. It sounds hollow in this white-walled room.

'Read your typed statement with a few additions and alterations. One of the thieves has confessed but they weren't working alone. We'd like you to help us catch the second and find the Infinity-Glass.'

'OK,' I say. 'But what if it doesn't work?'

'We have a Plan B. Elle, you've been through a lot and helped us solve the crime. If you are unable to speak, we fully understand.'

I take a deep breath. 'I WANT to speak,' I say. 'It's the right thing to do.'

∞

The private view's taking place in The Present Gallery at the Museum of the Past, the Present and the Future. It's a large white square room full of Anno's Olympic sculptures. My favourites are the sprinter on the start line, the shot putter mid-turn with one foot off the ground and the Paralympic high-jumper, suspended mid-air just after take-off. There's a large TV screen on one of the walls and a black glossy lectern in front of it.

The room's buzzing with people in posh clothes. Anno's wearing a full-length dress that looks entirely made out of litter and her hair's sculpted like the Leaning Tower of Pisa. I can't take my eyes off it. She smiles at me as I walk past and says what sounds like, 'Something to finally something your poem,' but it's too noisy to catch it in full. Anon wears a long pale pink silk dress with a matching walking stick and glasses; and even Nona, Evil Nine, looks smart in a dark blue trouser suit. There are lots of official gallery people, two men in wigs who look like they've leapt straight from 1752 and a frowning boy in a tall top hat. Would you believe, The Grandfather! He gives me the cat's eye and I look away. I'm amazed he has the nerve to attend this event, pretending to be a respectable citizen. And some of the

194

guests are plain-clothes police from the Bissextile Investigation Division but I'm not sure which ones!

Mrs C Eckler comes over to me. 'Are you still OK to read?'

'Yes,' I say.

'Your friends are here!'

She points to the entrance: Big Ben, GMT, Kwesi and MC^2 wave and come over.

'Mrs C Eckler filled us in,' says MC^2. 'You OK, Elle? Ain't no joke bein' arrested.'

Big Ben squeezes my hand. I can see he's barely slept. He must have been so worried about me.

'I'm supposed to read my poem,' I say, then lower my voice, 'but I'm going to talk about the Infinity-Glass instead.'

Someone clinks a glass and the room goes silent. The older wigged man addresses us from the lectern.

'Ladies and gentlemen, poets and artists, I am Mr Coffer, founder of the Museum of the Past, the Present and the Future. We are gathered here today to launch On Your Marks, Set, Gone! by celebrated artist and sculptor, co-founder of the Music, Maths and Movement School, Director of Movement: Anno. The sculptures that surround us are exquisite but might I say, Anno, that your flamboyant attire is a work of art in itself.'

He gives a low bow and Anno bows back. I worry her Leaning Tower of Pisa hairdo will collapse and she'll look like GMT when she hasn't combed her hair. But it doesn't. I try to concentrate on her litter dress, looking at it out of the corner of my eye, but it's no good. I can only concentrate on the task ahead. My speech.

Butterflies lurch in my stomach. As his introduction continues, words like 'absence' and 'non-existent dates' stand out in his speech. I see Portia slip into the room, wearing a slate-grey tracksuit. She nods at me, gives me a knowing wink and I nod back. Suddenly, I feel nauseous with nerves. Deep breaths, I tell myself. If you can break into The Vicious Circle and cope with the smell in 1752, you can do this. You can do it, Elle!

'. . . To open proceedings, I would like to welcome Elle Ifíè, who will read her poem inspired by the Infinity-Glass.'

My heart almost leaps out of my chest but I somehow manage to reach the front of the room. My hand's shaking so much, the piece of paper I'm holding makes more noise than my voice.

'I was going to read my poem about the Infinity-Glass,' I pause. 'But I thought I'd talk about the Glass instead.'

There's some background murmuring and a note of surprise but I take a deep breath and continue.

'On Monday it was stolen from the 1752 Gallery during my school trip. That evening, I leapt back in time to try to catch the thief and get it back. I failed. But I know who the thief is.'

'Then name the culprit!' says Mr Coffer.

'The thief is the same size as me and is familiar with the school track at Intercalary International. They also have a habit of tilting their head to one side before they leap. Like you do, Portia!'

'You don't have enough evidence,' says Portia. 'Leaplings can easily look up information about your school. And lots of people tilt their heads. Doesn't make them guilty.'

'We have more evidence, from your own lips.'

There's a hush in the room now and everybody looks at Portia. Everyone except me. I can't look at her; it would be too painful.

Even though she confessed to the police, even though this was planned, it's still horrible accusing a friend in public. I take another deep breath.

'But now I want to talk about the second theft. I met the original owner of the Glass in 1752: Francis Barber, servant to Dr Johnson, the famous lexicographer.'

Several people in the room gasp. Not everyone knew the history until now.

'I was there just after the original Glass was stolen. The witness said the thief was a woman wearing a fine silk gown and carrying a stick, who disappeared into thin air. The description exactly fits Anon.'

Anon shakes her head. 'How dare you make this wicked allegation against me! I suspect Mistress Anna is behind this.'

'But something didn't fit. Another witness, Old Meg, described the thief as being in such a hurry that morning, she didn't say "how do you do?" or give her coins like she had the day before. And Francis himself said the woman who was constantly asking him about timepieces showed "no desire to greet the Master". Yet Anon is a close friend of Mr Johnson. She loves visiting him. What if it wasn't Anon but someone PRETENDING to be her?

'Portia would be in the ideal position to copy her aunt's speech but she wouldn't be able to fool Mr Johnson. Unfriendly behaviour gave her away.'

'So you're accusing me of BOTH thefts?' says Portia. 'What evidence have you got that I stole from Mr Johnson's house?'

'These,' I say, showing the sweet wrappers. 'Dropped just

outside the candle cupboard. Which reminded me of the sculptures you're working on. Identical sweet wrappers. Whoever stole the Glass had likely leapt from the Art Department at the Music, Maths and Movement School.

'The original Glass was returned to Francis. But the ancient Infinity-Glass is still missing. Or is it? Ladies and gentlemen, I know where the Glass is!'

The low rumble of chat whilst I've been speaking stops. Everyone looks at everyone else. Mr Coffer has gone red in the face, ready to explode. He can't cope with the anticipation.

'Elle, in the name of God, discover it!'

'It's in a safe place where no one visits, in a year no one wants to leap to.'

On the word leap, a rush of air. Someone in the room has disappeared but it's not a clean leap, which means they weren't focused, they were flustered and before they totally leave the room, I catch a glimpse of their leaning hairdo, their dress, a tornado of sweet wrappers, their face twisted with fury.

Not Portia.

Not Anon.

But Anno!

∞ Chapter 23:00 ∞

THE PRESENT

The room goes crazy.

Everything happens at the same time.

Big Ben whoops; Kwesi and MC² do a sign dance full of high-fives and finger-clicking; GMT says, 'Far out, man!'

Mrs C Eckler is by my side, checking I'm OK.

Two black-hooded figures appear either side of Portia and instantly luggage her away.

A quarter of the overdressed guests, who are undercover investigators, disappear on the spot.

The Grandfather smiles a vicious smile, takes his hat off his head and replaces it. Oh my Chrono! He must think I didn't mention The Vicious Circle because I approve of it! It's the exact opposite. I don't think I've seen the last of him.

And Mr Coffer shakes my hand so vigorously, I'm surprised I still have a hand left!

'Well, well, well,' he says, addressing the room. 'This is truly an historical occasion. Fear not. The thief will be apprehended.

However, it is now my honourable duty to—' His Chronophone begins to buzz violently inside his jacket. He takes it out, checks it and his white bushy eyebrows rise.

'Mr Coffer speaking. Yes . . . yes . . . bravo! . . . My word! . . . Forward it, if you please, madam . . . Are you certain it is to be disclosed to the public? . . . Very well. Indeed, I will do so to the company immediately!' He places his phone on the lectern in front of him, takes a handkerchief out of his front pocket and mops his brow.

'Ladies and gentlemen, the thief-takers have excelled themselves. I have, in the past minute, received intelligence that the thief has been captured, with the Infinity-Glass, in 2073, about to conceal it in a pyramid of plastic.'

That was a little too much information for my mind to process on top of the past few minutes. But I'm glad Anno has been caught. Mr Coffer's now tapping into his phone, facing the television screen. It clicks on but he's having problems with the next step. MC^2 disappears from beside us, reappears next to Mr Coffer, who smiles at him.

'Maybe you could assist me, young sir?'

After a few taps, MC^2 steps back as an image comes onto the TV. The entire screen is a multicoloured collage of plastic bags, bottles and packaging. It could be an exhibit in this room but thankfully it's not. This is landfill so large it can't fit onto the picture. Anno appears out of thin air to the left of the screen. She's almost completely camouflaged in her sweet-wrapper dress but her distinctive black stacked hairstyle gives her away. She dives so far into the hill of litter, she completely disappears and although she did wrong, I hold my breath, worried she'll run out of oxygen and drown. But half a minute later, she reappears clutching what looks like a column of litter, shakes it and there it is: The Infinity-Glass! She raises it to her lips like she's kissing it, turns around and freezes.

Four tall black-hooded figures!

Mr Coffer clicks his phone and the screen goes blank.

'Conclusive evidence,' he says. 'This is a crime of the past, the present and the future; an offence against the private individual, the institution and the planet! Such Anachronisms receive weighty sentences.

'It will please you to know that the artefact was instantly recovered by the Investigation Division and is being restored to its rightful home downstairs in the 1752 Gallery as I speak. Justice WILL be done.'

There's a hushed silence.

'In the light of these extraordinary events, it is my duty to prematurely close these proceedings. But before I do, on behalf of the Museum of the Past, the Present and the Future, I would like to present this young thief-taker,' he gestures towards me, 'with a token of our gratitude.

'We advertised a reward for whoever found the Infinity-Glass. Therefore, it is with absolute pleasure that I bestow upon you, Elle Ifiè, a cheque to the sum of ten thousand pounds!'

Mrs Zhong appears from thin air at his side holding a large envelope, which she hands to me as she shakes my free hand. Everyone starts clapping. At first, I don't know how to react, overwhelmed by everything happening at the same time. But as the applause gets louder, my smile gets wider. It's not the money I'm thinking of; it's the acceptance of my statement, the success of Plan A and the video of Anno, evidence that proves that MC^2 and I are innocent.

∞

When the room clears, I notice Anon sitting in a corner, her walking stick resting against the wall. I feel a lump in my throat.

'I'm so sorry about Portia,' I say, 'and Anno.'

She looks up at me through her glasses. 'I am deeply sorry too, but I applaud you for your superior sense of justice. I am doubly wounded. Portia has always been a ne'er-do-well but she's young and has a good heart. Anno is old enough to know better, but she did it for the advancement of learning, for the greater good. My sister accrued monstrous debts for the school by ordering everything from the future. I shudder at the number of noughts we owe. I understand she had no intention of sharing the profits from the sale of the Glass.'

'Is that why she hid the Glass in the future and left The Vicious Circle?'

'I believe so, Elle.'

'What will happen to the school?'

'It will thrive without her input, as you well know. Dear Samuel always tells me: MIND OVER MATTER. That is the motto for the Music, Maths and Movement School and if we practise it, we will overcome our current challenges. Some future projects are secure.

'And I suspect your future, Elle, will take you to new heights. As Shakespeare said, "To thine own self be true." I wish you infinite success. You have my number; do keep in touch if you desire it.'

'I will,' I say.

∞

'How can you spend the money?' says Big Ben.

We Infinites are catching up outside in the museum gardens, sitting on the grass beside flowerbeds that read 2021 in white on a pink background. It's another hot day.

'I'll divide it between all of us, £2,000 each. I couldn't have done it on my own.'

'That's so cool, Elle,' says GMT, 'but I can't spend it on the west coast in '68. I don't need it.'

Kwesi shakes his head and holds up his hand.

'I suppose you can't spend it in 2049 either,' I say. 'I guess we can keep it in the bank for emergencies.'

Big Ben frowns. 'You accused Portia but not Anno. Portia is good.'

'That's how we planned it with the investigators, BB. Portia was part of the act. She'd already confessed to the police but pretended to be shocked when I accused her. It was a set-up to make Anno react. It must have been very hard for her to set up her mum. Once Anno made a run for it, we had the evidence.'

'You did good, Elle,' says MC². 'Did you know about the landfill?'

'I didn't work it out at first. But after I realised Anno was guilty, I remembered her brother, Nano, telling Millennia he had provided a safe place to hide the Glass. And Millennia mocking him for dumping things people didn't want in a year no one wanted to visit. I wonder if they'll arrest him as well for illegal landfill AND being an accomplice to the crime?'

'Hope so, sis! ROOT FOR THE FUTURE.'

'ROOT FOR THE FUTURE,' we all say, bumping fists.

'Two Glasses, two thieves,' says GMT.

Big Ben shakes his head. 'ONE Glass, two thieves.'

'Yes,' I say, 'and ONE mastermind. Anno planned the whole thing and got Portia to do the first theft while she was giving her museum talk.'

'Is that why Anno was early?' says GMT.

'Yes. She timed it exactly and meant to attend The Vicious Circle Meeting straight afterwards in real time. But once Portia texted her someone else had got the Glass, she thought she'd best not attend. You know how vicious the Circle can be!'

'So, Anno was the missing Eight!' says Big Ben.

'Yes. She desperately needed money to pay off the school debts. She reckoned the sale of the Infinity-Glass would do it. Plus, she got reward money from Millennia for stealing the plain version of the Glass from Francis. She did wrong but I feel sorry for her. The Music, Maths and Movement School's so brilliant!' I pause. 'Anno never wanted to share the money with The Vicious Circle: the money was for a good cause. That's why she resigned.

'If Anno hadn't exited, Portia wouldn't be in The Vicious

Circle now. Portia totally regrets the theft. She confessed as soon as I was arrested. That's how the police knew it wasn't me. AND,' I add, 'she's the one who bailed MC^2.'

'She took her time. The Squared was celled up for days!'

'She had to get the cash together. She'll be found guilty but she might not go to jail. She was acting for her mum, not herself.'

Big Ben frowns. 'She can't be a double agent from prison.'

'If she's sent to Do-Time, she can still have visitors,' I say, changing my seating position to stop the pins and needles. 'Our job's not over yet. We have to break The Vicious Circle: Portia can help us do it.'

Kwesi signs and MC^2 translates:

'Good work, Elle. But when did you guess it was Portia that did the first theft and Anno the second?'

'Mr Johnson often tilts his head to one side. Credit to Big Ben. He reminded me of it in the Daisy-Chain, which reminded me of Portia, which reminded me of the theft video. But it took a while to make those connections.

'Then, just before I was arrested, Portia said something about not celebrating non-events. That made me think of Anno's exhibition of events that never happened. I also remembered Anno saying people got her confused with Anon. AND she mimicked Anon's voice in their office, remember, BB? That convinced me it was Anno who did the second theft.'

'I still got the first theft video on my phone. AND The Vicious Circle recording from under the table,' says Big Ben. 'Oh, I just got a text!'

'Who's it from?'

'Not sure. Wait . . .' He scrolls down. I stare over his shoulder like I always do, to help him read.

'It's to both of us.'

I check my phone:

Congratulations to Elle and Big Ben! You are now Level 2.

'Who do you think it's . . . ?' I notice the others are smiling from East to West. 'Is it from Infinity?'

'Guess so,' says MC^2, 'since we ain't sent it. And far as I know, no folks infiltrated The Infinites.'

'Do you think Infinity was at the event today?'

'Coulda bin. Who knows? Anyways, you an' Big Ben just got promoted again.'

'Can I get the tattoo now?' says Big Ben.

'No,' I say. 'You're not allowed to get one before you're 18. It's illegal.'

MC^2, Kwesi and GMT laugh. They're 4-leap +1, 17, but they all have the ∞ tattoo, which is a bit naughty.

'Then how do we get Level 3?'

'All in good time, bro,' says MC^2. 'Enjoy the moment.'

We do. We deserve it.

206

∞ Chapter 00:00 ∞

THE FUTURE

A year has passed. It's September the 3rd 2022, a Saturday, the last weekend of the summer holiday. When I go back to school on Monday, I'll be in Tenth Year. Like last year, I smile when I wake up. In 1752, this date didn't exist. I turn off the alarm on my Chronophone, noticing several message alerts. I look at the corner behind the television where the mushrooms used to grow from the damp patch and smile again. We used the reward to pay the overdue rent and finally, finally got the landlord to deal with the damp problem. But Grandma was still on at me like an endless advert.

'Now you can buy good clothes like that your friend GT!'

I DID buy some new clothes but Grandma wasn't impressed. They look exactly the same as my old ones, but bright white and bigger. Once I find comfortable clothes, I don't like to risk getting different brands.

Today, though, I put on the only outfit that's different to the others. It's a 1960s tracksuit, frayed at the cuffs and off-white with age but it fits me like it was custom-made. Although it's polyester which makes me sweat, mixed with wool which makes me itch, I still love it. It's very me! So far, I've only managed to wear it for an hour at a time before I have to change back into my usual clothes. Now, I comb my hair into the biggest afro in the world, pop the cassette into my new retro player and imagine I'm in 1968. This is time travel without the effort. Even Leaplings need a break!

We have an Infinites meeting with Portia later, at a location so secret I can't even tell YOU! She's been out of Do-Time a month now. We hoped she'd only get a fine but she got a sentence for stealing a priceless object. Thankfully, it wasn't a long sentence because it was her first crime and she was acting under Anno's orders. In the end, none of The Infinites visited her in prison in case we bumped into members of The Vicious Circle. That would have been a giveaway.

But now, Portia's back in that crime ring as a double agent. She reports to us every week. She's doing a great job pretending to be recruiting for Millennia's grand plan when, in reality, she's helping The Infinites to thwart it!

I check my texts. The first is from Portia confirming the meeting. I delete it to destroy the evidence and wait for her follow-up message.

The second is from Ama, and it's only two words:

Robot's ready!

Brilliant. Everything's going to plan.

The third text is from Francis! I'm excited. I've only heard from him a couple of times since our last visit.

Colonel Bathurst died and left me in his will my Freedom and twelve Pounds in Money!

Sent Fri 3 Sep 1756. 11:22.

Another leap year; another big change for Francis.

I text him back:

That's BRILLIANT news! Don't spend it all at once.

It's strange thinking of Francis being 14, the same age I am now. Even stranger knowing that if we visited a churchyard, we'd find his headstone. Dr Johnson's buried in Poet's Corner at Westminster Abbey because of his famous Dictionary; I wonder where Francis is buried? But right now, he's very much alive on my phone.

Now I can go to Sea!

I picture Francis some time in his future, on a ship where they use marine sandglasses to tell the time. I think of his own Infinity-Glass, customised by Kwesi and MC², travelling hundreds of years through time until it's locked in a glass case at the Museum of the Past, the Present and the Future. And I imagine what it would be like if time itself was turned upside-down so instead of travelling day by day into the future, we travelled into the past instead.

As a Leapling with The Gift, I can't CHANGE time, but I can move backwards or forwards through it. It suddenly hits me – I can travel to any year I want, any time, any place. But it wouldn't mean anything if I didn't have a goal and true friends to help me achieve it. I'm a Level 2 Infinite now; next step, Level 3. I can't wait.

My Chronophone buzzes. That was quick! No time to get

changed out of this itchy tracksuit. I just hope the meeting lasts less than an hour. I can't say where it will take place but I can give you a hint what it's about: the evil teens, Millennia's masterminds.

I concentrate hard on the place, date and time.

I close my eyes tight.

And I leap!

∞ Acknowledgements ∞

I wrote *The Time-Thief* during lockdown in the run-up to summer solstice 2020. That meant sharing a workspace with family members who each deserve a gold medal for tolerating my constant complaints about noise or the discomfort of headphones. What's more, they were my first creative sounding board. A heartfelt thanks to my husband, Jeremy, for that special Spring date to Dr Johnson's House, the historic object brainstorm and invaluable insights when I talked through my storyboard. Thank you so much, Valentine, for inventing the leap clash, reading an early draft and telling me it had 'good baddies'. And thank you, Solomon, for our lively discussions about character, plot and internal monologue; your writing inspires me always!

A big thank you to everyone at Canongate for continuing to publish and champion my writing with passion and diligence. Thank you so much, Jamie Byng, for recommending me for that inspiring morning of online readings at Notting Hill School. A very special thank you to my editor, Jo Dingley, for your instant enthusiasm for *The Time-Thief*, insightful comments and coming up with a title so perfect, my sole contribution was the hyphen. I'll miss working with you on Book 3! Thank you, Aa'Ishah Hawton, for helping put the book to bed. I look forward to working with you on Book 3! Thank you, Leila Cruickshank, for your forensic copy editing; Vicki Rutherford and Megan Reid for ensuring the schedule ran like a dream; Rafaela Romaya for overall art direction and another vibrant cover design and likewise Debra Cartwright for your dynamic illustrations.

A special thank you, Lizzie Huxley-Jones, for your in-depth and far-reaching sensitivity read and passionate enthusiasm for the book. It's been a pleasure working with you again.

Thank you to my agent, Simon Trewin, and your team, for your passion for dictionaries, for believing in the entire Leap Cycle and making me laugh out loud when I thought there was nothing in the world to laugh about. Thank you to my performance agents, Melanie Abrahams and Rochelle Saunders at Renaissance One, for continuing to work hard promoting The Leap Cycle in difficult circumstances. Your support cannot be overestimated.

Thank you to the sharers of 18th century knowledge: Helen Woollison, Deputy Curator at Dr Johnson's House, for answering all my queries and your interest in the project; and thank you to the front-of-house team for enabling me to contact you. Thank you, S.I. Martin, for alerting me to the marvellous online map of 18th century London and for the exquisite historical detail of your novel, *Incomparable World*. Thank you to the authors of the following books that were invaluable to my research: *The Fortunes of Francis Barber* by Michael Bundock; *Dr Johnson's London* by Liza Picard; *The Life of Samuel Johnson* by James Boswell; and *The Time Travellers* by Linda Buckley-Archer.

A very special thank you to my watchmaker, poet and songwriter friend, Geoff Allnutt, for making that 150-mile round trip to answer all my questions about valuable timepieces.

An equally special thank you to Chris Bonnello, novelist, special needs teacher, creative writing tutor and autistic advocate, for creating the *Underdogs* series; and for your regular, encouraging emails whilst I was writing *The Time-Thief*. You're my role model for a four-book cycle!

A huge thank you to the following friends, creatives, academics and fellow writers for their support, encouragement and solidarity: Bernardine Evaristo, Philip Pullman, Benjamin Zephaniah, Kim Zarins, Steve Tasane, Carolyne Larrington, Julia Forster, Katherine Rundell, Fleur Hitchcock, Frank Cottrell-Boyce, Michael Morpurgo, Faridah Abike-Iyimide, Ben Miller, Elle McNicoll, Sophie Anderson, Libby Scott, Christopher Edge, Anna James, Candy Gourlay, Leone Ross, Ros Barber, Sasha Dugdale, Stephanie Scott, Rosemary Harris, Emma Foulds, Rebecca Mandisodza, Catherine Jones, Stephen Goodridge and Sue Jones.

A heartfelt thank you to all teachers, librarians, booksellers, bloggers, parents and promoters on and offline who have continuously and passionately championed the Leap Cycle from the word go: especially Scott Evans, the Reader Teacher; Indigo Williams at BookTrust; Mathew Tobin at Oxford Brookes; Anne Boyere of the SCBWI; Ashley Booth; Aidan Severs; and many many others too numerous to mention but you know who you are, wonderful people.

A special thank you to Oliver Foulds for reading early drafts and every single published version of The Leap Cycle and giving me fantastic feedback. You're a star!

Most of all, I thank readers, especially young readers, for your questions and quotes, letters and tweets, illustrations and imaginations. You're the writers of the future!

© Lyndon Douglas

Patience Agbabi was born in London in 1965 to Nigerian parents, spent her teenage years living in North Wales and now lives in Kent with her husband and children. She has been writing poetry for over thirty years. Her first novel, *The Infinite*, Book 1 in The Leap Cycle series, was published in 2020. Like Elle, she loves sprinting, numbers and pepper soup, but, disappointingly, her leaping is less spectacular.

The Circle Breakers, Book 3 in The Leap Cycle series, is coming in 2022!